Winter Park Library

The Last Night
at the Ritz

Books by Elizabeth Savage

SUMMER OF PRIDE
BUT NOT FOR LOVE
A FALL OF ANGELS
HAPPY ENDING
THE LAST NIGHT AT THE RITZ

The Last Night at the Ritz

A Novel by

Elizabeth Savage

Little, Brown and Company/Boston/Toronto

FIRST EDITION

T08/73

Library of Congress Cataloging in Publication Data

Savage, Elizabeth.
    The last night at the Ritz.

    I. Title.
PZ4.S263Las [PS3569.A823]   813'.5'4   73-4764
ISBN 0-316-77144-9

Published simultaneously in Canada
by Little, Brown & Company (Canada) Limited
PRINTED IN THE UNITED STATES OF AMERICA

For my mother
Mildred Ridlon Fitzgerald

The Last Night
at the Ritz

1

My friend and I are very grand these days. We meet at the Ritz.

If our husbands are with us, we lunch downstairs in The Bar, a small room that fronts the Garden. They always show us to the same table there and they don't ask us what we want to drink — they know. If we are early — we are almost always early — they bring my clear-as-glass martini and they bring her Dubonnet and then while we wait we watch the sights flowing past the windows (there are some very strange sights these days) and we watch beyond the sights across Arlington Street, until we see Len striding down the Garden path. Then Gay's face lights.

It was not always so. When we were kids we met at the Hayes-Bickford in Harvard Square because, as they say now, the Square was where the action was, although in those days you never saw the action. In those days there was a lot of brass and braid around but you still looked twice at a sari. In those days Len was overseas, a word that choked us up although we used to joke about it. (Where does he get to go on leave? Why, Eniwetok Atoll!) While she waited, Gay lived in a grubby flat off Plympton Place and tried to cheer it up with paint and prints. I lived on the Hill with the guy who might very well have become my first husband, God forbid. You couldn't possibly have cheered up that cul-de-sac. The windows were scarfed with oil-film and the stairs were narrow and crooked, and I remember once that Gay stayed over and in the morning I offered her a Benzedrine and she was horrified. I didn't think it was all that bad — we both had to get to work.

Gay's never approved of me. But she's always loved me. The two things don't have as much to do with one another as some people think.

I thought the Benzedrine was nifty. It came in little cylinders and you sniffed them if you had a cold; then someone pointed out that they did more than that. My first job, if you call it a job, was at Mass. General where the young doctors knew everything, like how to obtain pills and pure medicinal alcohol, which leaves no hangover although it does strange things to your legs. It is so good that one is not allowed to buy it.

"Or hey," I said, "you want a Peppy Pill?"

The look she gave me.

In those days we had been at the Ritz just once, and I forget just why. Slumming, perhaps. Or showing Len off in his uniform. It was a long blue evening and we had a beer on Charles Street and then walked across the Garden. Gay and I had on linen suits. I am surprised when I see the snapshots because I don't remember the skirts being that long. It was a hot night that smelled of new leaves and popcorn. In front of the Ritz the big cars came and went.

"Why not?" Len said.

With an officer, you went anywhere. Gay had a sherry and I had a ward eight, which had not been popular for some time but was strong. The fellows had Scotch and soda, which is what knowledgeable fellows had. We had only one because one was all we could afford, and at that we pooled our loose change for the tip.

When we were outside again and the doorman tipped his hat, Len said, "I'm coming here again."

I forget who I was with.

We met at college. Doesn't everyone?

It was a little hick college up north and neither Gay nor I wanted to be there. We felt that we belonged at Smith or at Mount Holyoke, but there wasn't any money. Gay's folks had died young and legitimately; mine were glamorous and no good and, as my aunt pointed out, didn't have the sense to travel on different planes. At that, I was the luckier of the two, because Gay's grandparents had stopped being interested long ago, while my aunt was very interested and gave me good advice and hand-me-downs and was not benighted — once in a while when she sent my laundry back, she tucked in some Lucky Strikes. We both had scholarships.

One of the worst days in my life — and I've had a few — was the day I got off the milk train and looked across the switchyard to the squared towers of the yellow brick library. They'd lost my trunk on the train, and I couldn't find a cab. I was wearing the uniform that my aunt had assured me that girls wear: wool skirt, wool sweater and saddle shoes, but I had the wrong season. The sun was hot and bright, the leaves had not yet turned, and everyone else was wearing cotton frocks that nipped in at the waist and spectator pumps. Everyone else knew someone else, too. There must have been other freshmen on that train; I didn't know it and don't remember to this day how I got to Emerson Hall, that big wooden barracks of a dormitory, or who told me to what room I was assigned, or how I climbed the wide shallow stairs scooped in the middle without getting lost. But I found number 45.

The door was closed and I felt unwelcome. I didn't know whether to knock and wait or to barge in. What the hell, it was my room too. So I tossed my head (with that bad permanent) into the air, flung the door wide and entered into my kingdom.

A long skinny room with tall skinny windows; it smelled of varnish and it smelled hot. I suppose it was clean, but flies bumped at the panes and the oak desks were scarred and dark. And there, with a hanger in her hand, her eyes wide with fright and looking like a small stern doll, was Gay.

She told me later that what she was most afraid of getting stuck with was a field hockey personality who would fill the room with pals and tennis socks. The wrong roommate, during those first weeks, could be pretty gruesome and the dorm was filled with the sound of weeping and the banging of doors as the girls rushed off to the dean of women. But I was not about to fill the room with pals. What I needed was one of those battered desks for my typewriter (the keys stuck and I had to keep the ribbon oiled; you can keep a ribbon going a long time with Three-in-One, although it makes a lousy carbon), a deep drawer for my notebooks and a roommate who would never peek at them. In those days I still thought I was going to write. What Gay required was order, and silence when she was working. Well, she got the silence.

Nobody ever understood why we were friends, not even people who came to know us well; not even Mary Hastings of the English department, whom we adored. Gay was neat, serious, organized and efficient. I was not. She was a natural respecter of rules and regulations; every time I turned around, one ruptured. She kept her underwear in clean piles in closed drawers; I hurled mine under the cot and washed them when I took a bath. If you kick up a suds everything gets clean, though Gay does not believe it to this day. Mary Hastings said that Gay would be better off for a little of what she called my *joie de vivre,* and that perhaps some of Gay's dedicated regard for scholarship would rub off on me.

This did not happen. But what we shared from the start and what, we felt, distinguished us from the peasants, was a deep reverence for the Word. And the companionship that sprang full-blown between us was not going to be shaken by quarrels — not real quarrels

— or hurt feelings or borrowed and laddered stockings or secrets betrayed.

Or by men.

Yesterday Boston was at its best. It's always at its best in May. The last forsythia still froths on the green, and the magnolia foams. The grass gives off that hot new smell and is starred with dandelions and the Pond is not yet soiled with gum wrappers. I came loping down the diagonal path, scattering pigeons and pleased with my small perfidious plan. When we were little and played tag or Red Light, if you didn't want to run you crossed your fingers and you called out "King's-X," and then no one could touch you until you were ready to run again. I was giving myself a whole day of King's-X. I suppose everything has to be faced in time, but you can choose your own good time to face it. Anyway, that's what I think.

So here I came, swinging my purse and easy in my flats. These kids don't know how hard it used to be if you were tall and the only flats you could find were loafers, which left something to be desired with evening dress. But that is not a problem anymore, and now that I am older my face has grown up to its bones and I think I look quite distinguished. My hairdresser is on to a good thing, too. She doesn't curl it anymore but sort of wraps it around my head, and it is still chestnut-colored without help.

I think I look different, but nice. Boston looks nice too, though different.

I've been away from Boston for a while and when I

am away, I miss the cobblestone streets and the brick-buckled sidewalks, the hedonistic couples on the grass, the gentle old men in the sun and the children shouting. They are all still there. But yesterday there was a rock group playing in the bandstand, a Hare Krishna bunch dressed in yellow cheesecloth chanted and danced and tossed their scalp-locks on their shaven heads, and in the high fork of a tree a very young man played a flute. Nice.

In the Fine Arts there is a painting (I think it is by Childe Hassam) of the Common on a snowy day. The ladies' skirts sweep the ground and they wear furs. The gentlemen wear hats. *A lonely cab-horse steams and stamps / and then the lighting of the lamps* . . . That was a nice time too, but a different season. I couldn't hear what that boy was fluting (maybe it was *Sumer is icumen in*) but he looked charming.

What was not so nice. I went up the little knoll to pay my tribute to the Union dead because I always pay tribute to the Union dead — I like the soldier, though the angels don't say much to me. I came right down again. There was a sad old man up there stretched on a bench with his terrible face exposed and his fly open. I wanted to close it, but I didn't. It would have looked strange if anybody saw; I certainly didn't want to be accused of tampering. And sure enough, when I was back upon the level a blue and white police car came driving right down the walk, which is something none of us would be allowed to do, and I felt suddenly thoughtful, which is not the way I had planned to feel yesterday.

But then a good thing happened.

I am superstitious. It's my belief that everybody is, but if you don't admit it, you can't take advantage. I take advantage. When in doubt I appeal to the higher powers — though never to the Highest. The Highest should be reserved for the time that really counts. But even among the lower echelons there are many powers, from Robin Goodfellow to Jupiter. I didn't like the way the grass on the Common was worn down nor the way the police car hesitated before it passed one reclining figure. So I mentioned it to Astarte, who for some reason is reliable in this kind of situation, and I pointed out that I would very much like a good day.

I was trying to explain this ploy of mine once to Sam — Sam is my husband — and he said, "You're just kidding yourself."

Of course I'm kidding myself. How else can you get along?

I think most people who marry like each other. You hear about the ones who fight a dirty fight, and there are always those pictures in the newspapers of the mad-eyed spouse who has really got rid of him or her. But most of us like each other. I like Sam fine. We haven't been married all that long, but I think probably we would have made it.

Anyway, about that one thing he's wrong. Right after I spoke to Astarte — everything changed!

At Charles Street I looked across to the iron gates of the Garden and the balloon man was still there and the popcorn vendor with his hot buttery bags, and the children. And the man with peanuts for the ducks on the swan-pond. The young men were flying kites and the young couples had puppies and babies and guess what! When I got to the bridge there was a little boy there who had two balloons and as I passed he said, "Here, lady," and he gave me the pink one. This year the balloons all have Happy Faces, which is all right with me. I can stand that much change. It was the good kind of balloon, the kind that tugs against the wind and not the kind that bobs on the end of a thin wand. I do feel that makes all the difference.

So I felt I would get my wish, which was that for one day everything would go the way I wanted it to go. I daresay it was selfish, but since I didn't wish anyone any harm, what's the odds? I felt so good, walking along with my balloon, that I started to sing a little song I sing when I am feeling good:

You can easily tell she's not my mother —

The young man who was supposed to be singing that song was definitely of the rakish variety and the object of his admiration no better than she ought to be. But fun. I always thought him rather a cad, so anxious he was that the good sport should not be confused with the better women in his life. No, no, she is not mother nor sister nor his own true love, but as he explains with a callous cheer:

. . . she's just a personal friend of mine!

The little melody is gay and bobbish, and I used to sing it to Charley when I was trying to get him to sleep.

Charley is my darling; he is not my son. He is Gay's son.

He certainly used to like that song. I stood there humming it on the far side of Arlington Street, waiting for the traffic to stop and watching the blue flags snap at the entrance to the Ritz and I thought, "It's going to work."

What I had planned. I have been staying at the Ritz alone because Sam's still out on the coast, and Gay and Len were meeting me for lunch, and there in The Bar, Wes and I had arranged to meet by accident. By accident because Gay has a way of being upset by my habits and while she never criticizes, I know when she's upset; her mouth tightens. I certainly didn't want our luncheon spoiled by a tight mouth.

I am not sleeping with Wes and I haven't for some time, and if I were going to I wouldn't do it at the Ritz, where I prefer to be registered only with my spouse. But Wes is fun and a very old friend, though one whom Gay instinctively distrusts. And what is a woman of my age doing with such thoughts? Well, people don't change much. I've always liked men; there's just something about them that pleases me. And though Gay's never come right out, I know that from time to time I have appalled her. But I did nothing to appall her while my husband lived. I mean the first one. The real one.

So here I came with my purse swinging, twenty minutes late (which would surprise no one), and carrying my pink balloon (which might surprise a few). You cannot wear mini-skirts at the Ritz — there used to be signs that told you so. But no one has ever taken a position about balloons. I don't suppose they thought the question would come up.

My spirits were high as the balloon. We were going to have a long lunch, and then Len would have to go back to the office and Gay and I would go up to my room and do what we have done these many years: commune. And meantime Wes would have slipped me the wink and we'd meet later for cocktails and oh, gee, kid!

The lobby at the Ritz is shaped like a narrow T and there is absolutely no place to sit down unless you want to go around one corner of the T, where there are two hard chairs by the door over which a sign proclaims: THIS IS NOT AN ACCREDITED EGRESS. A broad stairway circles up on your left and if Gay and I were alone we would meet up there, where there is a cavernous dark lounge and the Ladies' is tactfully hidden behind a big dark screen. The dining room is up there, too — all light and crystal and blue glass. This is a more appropriate place for ladies alone to meet because it is so proper. Sam was once sent back to his room to change from sandals into shoes.

But The Bar is more fun. I turned to the right there and looked into the mirror over the few stools where no one ever sits and saw what I expected to see.

Gay was waiting at our table, reflected in that mirror, caught in a frame and somehow for a moment suspended from time and particularly my own, like a portrait I could possess. She wore a thin white wool suit with something gold at the throat. For a little woman, Gay has great dignity, I think because of the way she carries her head with its cap of crisp gilt curls. She had her white ostrich-skin bag and looked very smart and removed. When Gay is unaware of others there is something about her expression that is very still and controlled and somehow, a little sad.

I called. She looked up. She smiled.

She is still very beautiful, my friend.

2

Len greeted me as if I were the one thing lacking in his life.

He is still most attractive, is our Len. His hair is still dark and still looks as if he had come in out of a high wind, and he has an unstudied look. But what always gets me, and Gay, and I daresay many another, is the look in his grey eyes, which is intense and totally directed. That and his manners, which are gentle and courtly in a way you don't see around much anymore. Also, he has a fresh and pleasant smell.

I haven't been in love with Len for a long time, although I like him with all my heart. But there was a time when one of those grey glances would turn my day upside down. It wasn't love, of course, but one of those overwrought, star-cross't attractions like that of Romeo and Juliet, who weren't old enough to love, either. How can you love anyone you don't know? At that age you have barely made acquaintance with yourself.

There was only one girl we knew that year who maybe was in love. She was a senior, she lived on our corridor, and it was widely bruited that she and her guy hadn't dated anyone else since their own freshman week. Doris was a warm, pleasant girl who would do anything for anybody. She was almost pretty, except that her nose was flat and broad. But having missed being pretty she settled for being kind and merry, which is not the worst settlement a girl can make.

Doris and her man were never seen apart, and wherever they were seen they were hand in hand. He was a hulking, friendly lout who was on the football team and Doris was small; he always looked way down at her as if she were something precious. They were the first pair that fall to get engaged. At Emerson Hall when a girl got engaged, they had a curious custom. The dining room rang with hysterical, if surrogate, delight. "Where, oh where is Doris Painter?" the girls sang.

Then Doris stood up, blushing. She had to stand. Not even the odd teacher who became engaged refused.

"She will wear a diamond ring!" the girls would triumph — if such was the case. Since nobody had any money in those days, the girls were more likely to be pinned. "She will wear a KDR pin!" in this case.

We were all green with envy until Doris Painter had her brain tumor. Not that anyone knew at that time what it was, because the local doctor missed it. She lay in the infirmary for what cannot have been weeks, although that is the way that I remember it. The school was not that inefficient, so I must be wrong. I do know that she lay there longer than another might have, because her parents were in Arizona. Her father had tuberculosis, a malady I never really thought existed, not off the Magic Mountain. Doris wished with such anguish not to worry them that they weren't notified, at least not right away. I don't suppose a few days would have made all that difference.

At first they used to let her come downstairs now and then to the smoking room, where she would sit joking and laughing, her big eyes hectic with fear. Much as we thought of her, it made us all uncomfortable, and presently we would all go wandering away.

And then on a February afternoon when the snow was falling in heavy fringe and tassels, I went to the infirmary with a list of assignments for a sort of friend of mine, who had developed flu in order to postpone a tough exam. This makes professors wild; they have to write new exams and use up all their questions. After all, what are you going to ask that's challenging and new year after year even about — say — *Lear*? I never pulled this stunt myself, which is no credit to me — I thought the second exam might be harder than the first. I would arrange it that way if I were the professor.

Anyway. When I was leaving Doris was standing in the door of her room, trying to get down the hall to the phone booth.

"Help me," she said.

So I helped her to the booth. By the time we reached it her breath was fast and shallow and she had to put her hands against the glass walls. Then she said urgently, as though it were important that I be reassured, "It doesn't hurt. It really doesn't hurt, not any more." And then while I tried not to listen, she at last called Phoenix. And then she called the KDR house, but she didn't reach her gentle oaf. Her small wasted face crumpled with disappointment.

When she was back in bed and I had just reached the hall again the phone in the booth began to ring insistently. Somebody else would hear it. Somebody else would come. I could not bear to feel again that birdlike body, how hot and weightless she had felt and how her arm trembled in the cup of my hand. I hope it was for someone else. I hope it wasn't the KDR house. Because I fled. And reached my own room shocked and shaken: like any proper poet I had from time to time been half in love with easeful death. Now, for the first time, I believed in it.

A friend of her father's came up from Hartford and Doris was taken by train to a specialist in Philadelphia, but she died before she got there. I don't know how I got thinking about Doris, and I don't think I shall think about her anymore.

But how, so quickly, did I get from love to death?

After all these years, I know when something's wrong with Len. That fine old intensity is still there but it seems somehow — how shall I say — turned inward, instead of out to the rest of us. When the waiter brought his drink, Len thanked him with all the old charm but as if his mind wasn't really on the drink, although the first one went down so fast and the second appeared so rapidly that I wondered if I were watching the beginning of some part of a new pattern.

And then I put the thought aside and addressed myself to my own glass. In a group, I always like to pace myself to the fastest drinker, especially when someone like Gay is along who may at any moment want to eat.

Gay and I never waste our visiting time on our own problems, so Len's presence interrupted no flow of confidences. He wanted to tell us about an author with whom he had conferred that morning, one of the Women's Liberationists — you'd know her name.

Len said she was a striking woman. "Or would be, if she weren't so afraid of being an object. What's wrong with being an object? There is no way she can be a disembodied sprite. *No way.*"

Gay and I looked at each other blankly. Like many old English majors, we don't hold staunch opinions about anything much but books. Or maybe it's not our training but our age. I don't know how Gay feels about Liberation. I don't even know how I feel and probably won't have time to go into it. I suppose we are often put down. But I don't mind recognizing that anatomically we are different; we are, and any fool can see it. What I don't like is terminology that assumes we are lacking in essential: everyone knows that a female rhyme ends in a "weak, feminine syllable." How about that! On the other hand there is at least one species of firefly (genus Phengodes, if you want to know) in which the male can't glow — it is the female who lights up. If I were male, I think I wouldn't want to hear much chatter about that. Live and let live, I maintain. We are all in this together.

"How's her book?" Gay asked with interest. "What did you tell her?"

"I had to say she'd missed the boat," Len said. "There

are too many of them." I think that Len meant books.

There is a short flight of steps that leads down to The Bar, and I was beginning to watch it with interest. It was not surprising that Wes was late; he is chronically late. But if he was too late he was still going to want his drinks, which would annoy Gay, or she was going to want to order, which would disappoint him. There didn't seem much health in it either way.

"Notice anything different?" That was our waiter, with the proud and ominous tone of someone who knows something that you don't know.

We looked around. There were the same round tables with the semicircular banquette seats over which a large lamp hangs which is indescribable unless you say it is like a huge Japanese lantern frozen into geometric angles instead of in the round. There was the same scattering of freestanding small square tables, including the choice ones by the windows where you could still watch the same people going by: the young girls with their long bare legs and the young men with their briefcases and the old women with their shopping bags and their small nervous dogs.

Len appealed to us. "I don't see anything different. Do you?"

The waiter bent to us. "Closer home," he said.

So we looked down at our own table and saw at once what he meant. There was no lion on our ashtray.

At the Ritz they are crazy about lions. There are gold lions on the blue flags that snap above the Arlington Street entrance and within, lions adorn napkins and coasters and ashtrays and menus and are embossed on the glossy cards and envelopes on which one is encouraged (as we found later) to write notes for friends who cannot otherwise be reached, or do not choose to be. The lions seem a dubious symbol of hospitality since they snarl and their tongues obtrude contemptuously. But we are used to them; they comfort us. Their manes foam around what is probably their shoulders. One cannot be sure, because their heads rest upon crowns; they are your run-of-the-mill British crowns, with a suggestion of fleur-de-lys. The lions suggest opulence, grandeur, and a touch of snobbery, which is exciting.

"By George," Len said indignantly, "you're right!"

"It's a new policy," the waiter said with the importance of one who is in on new policies. "The guests kept taking them."

I doubted this very much. Not that the guests kept taking them but that the management would mind. They are very indulgent to us at the Ritz and besides, think of the advertising. But Harold has been our waiter for a long time and we were not going to openly doubt his word.

With the deft gesture of waiters that I do so much admire he produced from nowhere a new ashtray upon which the familiar gold beast lowered. Then Harold murmured to me.

"If I was you," he said, "I'd take this one. That is, if you would like."

I nodded sagely. None of us laughed. Nobody likes anything to change.

I thought I probably wouldn't take the ashtray. I've already got one at home and am not going to have much use for another.

"Oh, tempera," Gay said. "Oh, mores."

So I told her about the one I had at home.

Len said, "What about one more?"

I stalled, watching for Wes and thinking how cheerful it would be to see him. When we were undergraduates I was as long-toothed about Wes as Gay is now, because Wes was a Business Major and knew too much about marketing. But later when he became an investment broker and before Len had anything yet to invest, I got quite fond of him because he arrived one night (out of the blue) bringing a bottle that at that time we couldn't have afforded, and fell asleep in Charley's playpen.

I thought that was nice.

3

How DO YOU KNOW when something has gone wrong with someone whom you like with all your heart? *Let me count the ways.* I counted the feather-lines around Len's eyes and mouth that I thought tension had brought, not time. I noticed the indecipherable expression with which he kept glancing at Gay: sometimes as if he were looking for her support, sometimes with hostility. Sometimes with something that I thought was guilt. Or fear. I know a little about them both.

There is something sad in noticing the first cracks in the self-possession of someone of whom you've been proud. It feels the way that I suppose kids feel when they see in their parents the first signs of age.

What we had admired about Len from the beginning was his self-possession. He had that quality that in those days we would not have called cool. Force that he didn't have to raise his voice to exert. Humor, but never had to laugh too loud. In fact, he had what in our salad days we used to see in heroes — strength with the capacity for tenderness. Or anyway, the illusion of it.

And even when that façade cracked — it did sometimes — we felt he himself cracked it; not something
from outside. Len always led from strength. No matter
what the new ladies think, that is a quality that most of
us find irrisistible.

Gay still does. Because she was watching him, too,
with all the old love in her eyes and — a word I had
never thought to use of Gay — slyly. I found it deeply
disquieting to sit there watching my friends watch each
other.

For a moment I was wild with Wes. Anyway, Len
gets places on time. And anyway, when Len makes
mistakes he doesn't hedge his bets — he makes them all
the way.

I know, because Len and I once made a mistake. We
made a big one.

That first year, we had to take either a math or a
science. Gay could add and subtract and she could even
do long division, and the first thing Mary Hastings
liked about her papers was that they were sound. Gay
was exempted from freshman English and elected calcu-
lus; she said it wasn't a bad thing to know. I had a
secret even then that I didn't tell Gay — I was a freshman under false pretensions. In those days you could
bypass the College Boards if you were certified by your
high school, and someone at my high school had made a
fine mistake — the C I got weeping and wailing and
cheating every inch of the way in algebra had been
recorded as geometry, which was a requirement. I didn't

tell Gay because she would have thought I should have gone straight to the office and confessed. I knew I couldn't pass geometry.

I still think I was right. On the placement exams Gay and I were the only ones who could explain "Prufrock," and even Gay didn't notice that Eliot had nodded: Let us go then, you and *I*, when the evening is stretched out against the sky . . . I was not likely to ever need geometry. I chose geology.

I liked it, too. We drew attractive charts of syndromes and synapses and learned singing words. Lepidocrocite, for instance. Carboniferous. But two important things I couldn't do. I couldn't for my life compute the speed with which an earthquake moves, assuming that it starts in Sacramento, and on field trips when we looked for glacial boulders and for scour, I couldn't face the cows. Len was in my class. He didn't give a damn for cows.

This one particular cow breathed deep at me across a narrow brook and then huffed and splashed toward me. You can say what you like, I still think that cow was rabid. Len caught my hand and pulled me up the bank and we missed everything the instructor was saying about till.

Later he tipped me the wink and we vamoosed.

No, of course that isn't what we would have said. It is my aunt who would have said vamoose.

I have a snapshot of my aunt at about the time she would have said it. It was taken at Paragon Park and she is wearing bloomers and a middy blouse. Her hair is in a heavy braid. She is smiling triumphantly and holding up a Kewpie doll and she looks very pretty and very lewd. I wish I had known her then.

I do wish I had known her better. When I was very little she took me once to Loew's Theater. Some one sang "Red Sails in the Sunset," and I was embarrassed because when everybody sang (as we were urged to do) she sang right along: "Oh, bring back my loved one . . ." and even back then I knew her loved one had vamoosed. I couldn't imagine singing about it in a public theater, but for some reason it seemed to ease her. Afterwards, we had lunch at Schrafft's.

So Len and I vamoosed.

It still bewilders me the way fellows I didn't even notice then have turned out to be the vice-presidents of life insurance companies, when at the time they didn't know a gerund from a gerundive. But you had to notice Len. He was even tall enough for me, and his dark eyebrows climbed his forehead on a slant, and under them there were those grey eyes. When he caught my hand in his long strong hand, it was like an electric shock.

"Relax," he said. "That cow doesn't trust you, either."

Which is the story of my life. Nobody — except for Gay — has ever trusted me. And for good reason.

By the time we got back to town I was in love, the way you are in love at seventeen . . . heart knocking, clammy hands, racing pulse. We stopped for coffee.

In that town, that in October looked like a calendar with gold leaves drifting underfoot and every now and then a scarlet leaf stumbling down an aisle of air, there was nothing to do but to neck or to drink coffee. The coffee was usually bland and milky and served in porous mugs that made you look sharply for the traces of somebody else's lipstick. But we drank a lot of it. We drank it at a joint called Chuck's under a cold blue fluorescent light because at Chuck's the jukebox had "The Lady Is a Tramp." We drank it between classes at a strange little place across the railroad tracks because the jukebox there had "Bei Mir Bist du Schoen." But mostly we drank it at Park's Diner, where they must have figured that many a mickle makes a muckle, because they let us take up a lot of space for a dime's worth of coffee and an order of buttered toast.

"What are you going to do later?" Len asked.

I explained confidently that I was going to write.

"That's great," he said. "I'll publish you. I'm going to be an editor."

He was, too. As it turned out, he had an uncle in the firm, but even uncles can't help unless you're good at it. Len's very good at it. When it comes to prose he has what in a singer you call perfect pitch.

"Thursday night?" he said.

But by Thursday night I was campused.

I understand it's all different now and the boys and girls all live together on odd and even floors. But I think our school was rigid, even for those days. Freshmen had to be in at seven-thirty except for one late-night a week, when we could roam at will until the giddy hour of ten. We signed out and we signed in, and woe betide you if you didn't go to the library if that is where you said you were going. The assistant dean, Miss Agnes Wurlitzer, hovered while you signed in, and if she got a whiff of a beer breath, it was curtains. She also checked the vestibules. Wednesday night I got caught necking in the vestibule.

The way it worked out, there was always a girl on bells, and when your date came she rang your floor and then somebody hollered. I couldn't face it. In those days I allowed myself some leeway; everyone knows writers need experience. I could have faced doom and disaster (disaster has both dignity and dog) but I couldn't go down those worn steps and meet Len under the bald light of the hall and explain to him that I was in-nights for smooching with someone on the football team — second string, at that.

"You go," I said to Gay.

He took one look at her, and that was that. Or that was almost that.

Believe it or not, it wasn't all so different in those days. We didn't call them hangups, but we had them. We knew a girl who threatened to jump out of the third-story window because nobody loved her, but I suppose everyone remembers one of those. Another kept insisting that she had peasant blood and was born up to her ankles in manure. That girl blamed all her troubles on the fact that her father liked to go to bed with her mother and liked to go to bed with his mistress, I mean at the same time. Well, I suppose that would be confusing. She called the town she came from Vermont's Tobacco Road and we saw no reason to dispute it, although I met her mother once and she looked just like anybody else to me. And there was a curious little squat girl from Hong Kong who was said to be very rich (how else could she have gotten all the way here from Hong Kong?). She wore a trench coat in all weathers and certainly had some kind of hold over her roommate, who was blond and very pretty and didn't dare to date anyone. Gay and I both read *The Well of Loneliness*, and I thought the idea intriguing, though not my cup of tea. Gay jumped the next time I brushed up against her. Well, I just wondered. But it wasn't her cup of tea either. Believe you me.

But mostly what caused havoc in the dormitory was girls who slept with boys, or at least wanted to be known as someone who had slept with a boy. We didn't. I don't think we were more fastidious, we were just more scared. We both knew about condoms; we also knew they didn't always work. Well, they could have holes. And we knew there were girls who had abortions, but we wouldn't have known where to look for an abortion. Every town was supposed to have some old dirty doctor who would do it, but nobody I ever knew knew a dirty old doctor. Everyone I knew who got caught got married, but only after a lot of tears and a lot of snotty remarks from the dean.

The dean didn't always know what was going on. There was one girl on our floor Gay and I sort of liked until we decided that she was impractical beyond belief; she wept every thirty days because every thirty days she thought that she was pregnant and we sympathized at first, but then it got monotonous. We didn't so much mind her constant pregnancy, but we didn't like the fact that her man took pictures of her getting pregnant and then showed them around. It seemed to us that was wrong.

And then there was the girl who always did it under the grandstand, which seemed crude. We thought it sounded damp, and there would be bits of old tickets drifting down and cigarette butts probably, and bottle caps, and we wondered how she could keep her mind on anything. It seemed very gauche to us. Which is why it was so awful when I thought that I was pregnant. I couldn't tell Gay, because it was a coarse and thought-less thing to do, and I certainly couldn't tell her why it happened and I certainly couldn't tell her who it was. It was all an awful mistake.

The worst of it was that during spring of our freshman year Gay and I were being better than anybody else. We happened to know a good woman and had decided we would like to be good women too, because every-where this woman went, she exuded goodness like a fragrance. Well, she was temperate and loyal and com-passionate and strong and she bore burdens with great grace. She was also very lovely. She had a wide white smile, blue steady eyes and black hair ever so brightly stroked with silver. And she had slim arms and a sweetly sagging tummy that bespoke the generosity of childbirth. Then her difficult husband lost his job in spite of all our protests and petitions and she went away with him, with all her children clutching at her knees, and she still smiled, which really cracked us up.

So we decided that is what we wished to be: better women.

I'm sure all the girls we didn't like and who didn't like us must have been astonished. We listened to everyone's complaints and allowed others to precede us in the shower stalls. We stopped making cracks about others' eating habits and IQs, and we were very careful to keep all the rules because we understood how difficult it all was for the dean, but we did not condemn the transgressors, because who knows another's need?

It was a lot easier for Gay than it was for me, because she was born with a certain equipment for it — namely, temperance and gentleness and strength and (I think) not much temptation, at least not at that time. I think I knew from the beginning that it was not going to prove my natural bent, but I did try.

It lasted almost a whole week.

What happened was that we both had a Chaucer paper due. When Gay worked her eyes glistened with the pleasure of it, and Sherlock Holmes could not have pursued Moriarty with the intensity with which she tracked down a cross-reference. She had chosen some significant, acceptable theme; in a panic, I elected Chaucer and Spring, and drew little flowers and lambs in the margins to show how I felt about Chaucer and Spring. (Mary Hastings said it was charming, but not sound.) Watching her speed and order, I got downright scared. We were all supposed to keep those little cards and Gay always kept them and what's more, remembered why she had written on them what she had written. She knew how many spaces to go in from the margin and what item comes first in a bibliography. And all this time she was unbearably long-suffering.

The papers were due on Monday, and it was a great relief when Gay woke up snapping and snarling on Saturday morning. She didn't want to go to breakfast and didn't thank me for the coffee I sneaked back to her; she said it was cold, and she said that if the freshman down the hall needed loving support tonight she knew where she could look for it. And then Len called, all excited. He had a friend who had an aunt who had a cottage at the lake and the aunt, a most respectable person known throughout the town for her good deeds and sobriety, had called the dean and arranged for us to be her house guests. Gay wouldn't even talk to him.

So I went.

But first I gave her every chance. I pointed out that our idol had put her husband before all things, and Gay said that Len was not yet her husband. I reminded her that men have delicate egos. Gay said she had a delicate grade going in that course. I said that Len had gone to a lot of trouble to arrange this weekend, and Gay said, not enough to have inquired whether or not she was busy. So then I asked her if there was anything I could do, and she looked up from her typewriter and her texts and her carbon copies and she said yes, that there was one thing I could do.

Nobody has to take that sort of thing.

I have always had a passion for lakes, which I think began when I was a very little girl and first saw the Wading Pond in the Common. There was something about that brown water, all so clear and quiet, and of course when you are little you don't notice that it nudges against cement. And maybe people didn't used to throw peanut shells into it — anyway, I don't remember peanut shells.

Lately, with Sam, I've learned to know the real lakes, the high lakes, the wild ones. Sam is very big for the out-of-doors and every summer since we have been married (which is not really all that long), we have high-tailed it for some mountainy place. The first year we went to Tahoe which you might as well forget, because you can't see the water for the water-skiers. The next summer both his kids wanted to go to Europe, and we pretended that he didn't mind. We went to Montana, to a place called Seeley Lake where you had to hire a car and driver because on your own, you probably wouldn't make it. When you got there you pumped your water by hand and rowed across the lake for your supplies and hoped to hell you hadn't forgotten anything because there wasn't anyone to borrow from, not for miles. That lake was a clear cup in the fist of the Rocky Mountains; tall tamaracks towered against an abandoned sky and at night, mountain lions screamed. It was cold for swimming because of the glacial streams that fed the lake, and where they chuckled into the quiet water we kept our milk. The pebbled beach hurt your feet.

I remember that one time we had guests. They brought a child, which we had not expected them to do. After the drinks and the laughter and the steaks and the moment when the wood range got too hot and glowed like a ruby, the mother couldn't find the outhouse. All the men had to accompany her up a steep path that was slippery with needles and wait there, with their flashlights tracing hilarious patterns through the treetops while she went. Much later, I heard the child crying in the night.

It was late, very late — no, it was very early, and I wasn't very tight. For some reason, I had not got very tight. So I groped for my sneakers and didn't find them and I went barefooted out on the big screened porch and I said, "Sshh."

She put her head up like a little turtle.

Beside her on another canvas cot her mother's mouth was slack and open and her breath sour.

I beckoned. I said, "Want to come?"

No, I don't think I was taking much of a chance. Daylight was paling behind the high peaks and when we pushed the rowboat from the shore you could hear the grate of the pebbles and the single drops falling from the oars. I didn't take her out so far that I couldn't see the rocks slanting and shimmering beneath the hull. Then way across the water ripples began to shine and a fish leaped and snapped and we drifted, and when I feathered the oars the silver circles spread. Then a loon cried. And then, first above the ranges and then upon the foothills, feather by golden feather, the sun came up.

And then the mosquitoes began to bite. She was a skinny little kid, not a pretty child, not even a very appealing one, and the only contribution she made to the conversation was to tell me at one point, "Grownups smell bad." But when we came up the piney path to the cottage she was grinning, and her cold little hand was fast in mine.

There was a smell of bacon and of coffee on the chill crystal air. No one was awake but Sam, but he was waiting for us on the steps.

"What about a pancake?" he asked.

And later over our tin cups and eggy plates he looked at me with his nice level eyes.

He said, "I'm sorry it's too late."

He meant I should have had a child.

I said, "It's all right, Sam. Honest."

What I didn't tell him was that, in a way, I have had Charley.

That lake near the college was domestic and intimidated, but it was pretty just the same. April was bad in that town; the gutters ran with cold slush and the dank air held the exhaust fumes low, and the sour smell from the paper mill. Once out of town the pasture grass was sweet and in the Kennebec the ice had broken and the logs from the lumber camps were piling up against the posts.

The hills around that lake rolled low, then there was a thin fringe of white birch, and then when Len's friend stopped the car you could hear the breeze rattle the new leaves and the small lap of ripples on the little shore. Snow still crusted lacily under the trees and when we found a bench and tried to sit, our bottoms dampened. It was late afternoon. A pink light stained the pale water, and the first frogs were peeping.

There was no aunt, of course.

At least, there was no aunt in the cottage to which we

had the key; the friend of Len's friend was a good mimic. I think I'd known it all along, but if I'd admitted it, even to myself, Gay would have sensed it. I hadn't really given her every chance.

It was too little for a proper lake and all these squatty cabins circled the place like Ring-around-the-Rosy. The doors were all boarded up and the shutters were nailed on, and when we got into the one which was the aunt's, we opened the windows up, first thing of all. The power wasn't turned on, of course, but there were kerosene lanterns that blossomed in the dusk; their interesting stench fought with the scent of the new shallow grass.

And then the fire. The cottage was damp but the birchwood was dry and flamed up in a moment and sent the shadows prancing, and the sweet woodsmoke hung heavy against the sweet mist rising from the water. We cooked our hamburgers and opened up our bottle — a whole pint for the four of us; imagine! — and then we stacked our plates and Len's friend said we would scour them in the morning at the water's edge with sand. Then the fire laughed and the boys turned down the lamps. There was a brief sudden shower.

And then our friends began to neck. They were so beautiful and they were bone fide; her picture had been in the *Evening Sentinel*. They would be married in June and the invitations were engraved already, although they had not been addressed. They lay there by the hearth with their lumber jackets on and their boots off and they touched one another, very gently. He lifted her head with one hand and with the other he slipped a pillow under it and her hair spilled amber in the firelight.

So when Len's friend said, "There are only two bedrooms. Would you mind?" what else were we to do?

The bed was rackety and the thin sheets limp and cold and for a little while the rain slipped quietly against the windowpanes. I knew Len wanted Gay with him, but I was the one who was there. After a while, the peepers peeped again.

. . . *who will stand between me and the crying of the frogs?*

Nobody.

Gay's paper was pristine. I've never known anyone who can fit pages into a folder so evenly. Her pagination was perfect and her reference cards all filed away for future use. Her footnotes were blinding in their accuracy and her bibliography a joy to behold if bibliographies happen to give you joy.

"Listen," she said, "I'm sorry, but I did have to get it done. What's she like? Was it fun? Do you think Len would like to take a walk?"

"Why don't you ask him?" I said sullenly.

And a few weeks later, you can imagine how we felt.

It was wrong, up one side and down the other, and I was out of love with him and he had never been in love with me, and here we were maybe: stuck.

We really didn't know much in those days. I had heard that if you shook a Coca-Cola bottle up it might help, but even I wasn't ignorant enough to see how that could help. Len said he would ask around and I said that he certainly wouldn't: they would think he was asking because of Gay, and of course that was exactly what they would have thought. I had enough to cope with without thinking the guys were tittering about Gay.

Len said he understood that girls were late sometimes just because they were nervous and I told him that indeed, I was very nervous. I am a person who believes not only that you can change the future but, to some extent, the past. If you elect to wipe out what has happened, pay it no mind, give it no room in your consciousness — why then, it didn't happen. I had decided to wipe that weekend out. For one thing, I wasn't very pleased with myself and for another, my romantic interest in Len was waning rapidly. But it would be hard to do if there were visible consequences. Of course I was nervous.

Len said that if the worst came to the worst we could marry. I told him over my dead body. By now I was beginning to wonder what Gay saw in him.

Then he came up with an idea. Someone he knew held the theory that you combined a scalding bath with getting drunk on gin; I cannot imagine why this was supposed to help. But he smuggled me a pint of gin and suggested that I try getting drunk, and one wet afternoon I tried it. I didn't want a child and besides I had never been drunk and wondered what it would be like. And I certainly didn't want to marry Len.

I don't remember very much about that whole thing. I do remember those revolting johns. There was one on each floor, designed to more or less meet the requirements of some forty girls, and one was no more attractive than the next. In each there were rows of basins where the girls put up their hair; before you used one you looked aside while blindly, with a wad of toilet paper, you wiped out the hairs and the gummy rivulets of toothpaste. There were two showers and two tub stalls. For some reason the shower stalls didn't lock; you signified your presence by running the hot water until the steam drifted above the partition. The tub stalls had bolts. If you were lucky enough to get one first you bolted the door and the others could complain all they liked but as long as that door was bolted, you claimed sanctuary.

Mostly, the girls wanted to tub just before dinner so they would be fresh for their dates. I sneaked in about two o'clock. I had the gin in a small rubberized bag that was supposed to hold bobby pins and rat-tailed combs and such, and I was scared. Reason tottered at the thought of what would happen if one were caught drinking — and with purpose and enthusiasm — in the dormitory; perhaps you would be pelted out of town with ink bottles and erasers. And there was always, on every floor, a few pinched maiden types whose sole desire was to see that standards were kept up. On the other hand, other prospects frightened me even more. What did you do if you were going to have a child — I mean, what did you *do*? How could you hold your head up? How could you feed it? How could you keep your scholarship?

The gin was horrid. I had taken the precaution of bringing a Coke to cut it with, but naturally I hadn't thought of a glass. And didn't dare to waste any of the gin — it might be that just that one swallow would make all the difference — so I slugged the first of it down straight and then tried to pour the Coke into the gin bottle. The warm Coke didn't help the warm gin all that much and after a while it got harder to pour, too; a lot of the Coke went into the tub, which seemed to me exquisitely funny. I giggled and eased the Coke bottle down upon the floor. I've forgotten a lot about that bathroom — the washbasins were on the left, but where in the world were the hoppers? They must have been there, but I can't see them. And were the windows curtained? They must have been, since there was always one girl who was hysterically convinced that she was being watched by some man with binoculars. But I can see to this day the floor beside that tub and the Coke bottle balanced on a crack in the mottled brown linoleum.

Gay said it was a wonder I didn't drown.

She had come back from class and found me gone and wondered about it, since I had pleaded a paper to type. And then she noticed that my bathrobe was gone, which explained everything except why I was away so long. After an hour she got uneasy.

I don't know how she got me out of that tub. I do know she had to crawl under the stall door in order to do it. If it had been anyone but Gay the fat would have been in the fire. But her honesty was so well-known, her integrity so widely recognized that if we met anyone in the hall and she said she was helping a sick friend, that friend was sick. I think even Miss Wurlitzer would be persuaded. It was just like that old wheeze about the wife who demanded "Would you believe your cussed eyes before you believe your honey-bun?"

I don't even know how she did it physically, because she's such a small person and I'm a great long-legged thing and even then, to put it prettily, was well-rounded. But she managed, and never had at me about it later, either.

It was dark when I came to. I was in my narrow bed and in my bathrobe and the sheets were wet because the bathrobe was wet. Have you ever waked at the wrong time of day, when others are pursuing their innocent decent ways? It is not comfortable. My stomach was swaying and my head felt soft and swollen; outside the door I could hear clean healthy laughter and the rat-tat-tat of high heels coming up the stairs. Since they were coming up the stairs and since nobody wore high heels except going down to dinner, it was after dinner.

I also knew that Gay had had no dinner, because when I clicked my eyes I saw her sitting at her desk in the same twin-sweaters and saddle shoes that she'd had on when she left for Romantic Revival. I moaned and she looked up right away.

I said "Jesus. I reek." And then I said, "I'm sorry, Gay. I guess I passed out."

She denied it.

She swung around in her chair and pointed at me with her pencil and she denied it. She said fiercely, "You did not pass out. You fainted."

But it was years before we laughed about it.

So that is the story of my first lopsided love affair.

And it explains, I guess, why after that I always made sure that if there was any lop, the lop came on the other side. Curiously enough, Len and I became good friends. I suppose there is no tie that binds like a shared (and escaped) disaster. At any rate, that is a mistake we never made again.

No, I don't think it was the gin that did the trick.

4

OH YES; I know Len well enough to know when something's wrong. I don't claim that I knew what. But there was something restless about him and his eyes under the slanting brows were a bit too quick catching the waiter's eye. It could have been a maverick author, or perhaps his stocks were down. I mean way down, because he was a knowledgeable buyer; you don't frequent the Ritz on random stocks and bonds. But under the easy chat he wasn't really with us and the warmth of his voice didn't match his eyes. His grey eyes were as bleak as those of someone who has just said, "Well, thank you, doctor," and then has stopped at the desk to make arrangements.

Remember that I hadn't seen either one of them for two years. At our age, a lot can happen in less than that; it doesn't take any time at all for the axe to fall.

Gay did look tense and tired. But then, I'll bet Gay was born looking tense. In Gay, tension is attractive and a bit intimidating, because she always looks as if she knew something the rest of us don't know yet, and one feels that she will spare us just as long as she can.

And then a cold thought hit me. Casually as I could, I asked my friends, "How's Charley?"

Len frowned.

I suppose I feel that Charley is the child I didn't have that time. Don't make too much of it — I haven't been honing for Len all these years. But I never did get around to having a son of my own. Barry and I were having too much fun and there seemed to be plenty of time — then suddenly there wasn't any time at all. Sure, I've been married since, but not to anyone with whom I wanted to bear. A woman who dislikes me (there are those who dislike me, somewhat to my surprise) once suggested that my childless state accounts for my continued interest in fun and games. Maybe so. But I have never felt deprived. Not since I went to see Gay in the hospital (it seemed so unlikely to me that one of us should have proved gravid) and she looked up at me and told me, "He's a boy."

Charley doesn't look on me as a mother. But I look on him as a son.

But Gay's voice gentled and she said, "I think Charley's doing fine."

So that wasn't it.

It's a mistake to pry, and a mistake I never make on the first two drinks, nor after the third. One does have to watch that third. Yesterday I was spared, because when Gay began to look pointedly at the menu I was able to say, "Well, for cat's sake. Look who's here."

Wes had strolled in with a newspaper folded under his arm, the way you do when you don't expect to have anyone to talk to over lunch. I admired that bit. One of the reasons that Wes is part of my fun and games is that he plays along so well and likes disguises. Wes is not a handsome man, but he has a certain *panache* and a kind of insolence that I find attractive. Well, like once many years ago when I first started seeing him, we were stopped for speeding. He had an MG that year — I mean one of the first squared off, low, good ones, and he looked up at this cop character and popped his rather prominent eyes and said, "What are you — some kind of a safety nut?" I thought that was nice.

Gay doesn't care for Wes because she thinks he's a lightweight, and when I point out that lightweights don't get trusted with all that money, she is not convinced. What she really doesn't like is that he's married. Now, really. Dorothea is vindictive about a lot of things, but not about me. She has known all about me for years and couldn't care less.

Len was tickled to see Wes; I thought he would be. For one thing, they like each other. For another, it's hard to talk Gay into a third Dubonnet (I don't blame her — who'd want a third Dubonnet?) but when a friend joins you it is only courteous to order all around.

"Well, honey!" Wes said, and he was so delighted and surprised that I could hardly believe we'd been talking just an hour before. "When did you get into town?"

But Gay wasn't fooled. She slid me a little look and then she smiled. One of the nice things about Gay is that she doesn't get testy if you don't live up to what she feels is right. She wishes that I would live up, but that's because she loves me. She thinks I'd be happier if I were pure at heart. But I think I am pure at heart: there are all sorts of ways of being pure.

Wes hasn't kept up his tennis and he has a tendency to roll above his belt, but he has a good face starred with laughter lines, and he has had his troubles. Gay knows that and she sympathizes. She just can't understand why he's not more serious about them.

My poor friend: she is so good and so grave.

And so vulnerable. She really thought she knew just how it's done. First you work hard and thoughtfully and win all the prizes. Then you marry your true love and live passionately forever after. And your children call you blessed because simplicity and discipline and truth gird you in triple brass.

It isn't all that simple.

You are going to say that I am jealous, and perhaps I am — it is an idea that I have entertained. But I think I love my friend, and I think I honor those fine and wholesome notions that she has. I just haven't found them practical. In my book, it also takes a little laughter.

I don't think I understood Gay one bit until the spring vacation of our sophomore year, when I was left high and dry because my aunt was off somewhere with friends. Knowing her friends, it must have been a whole heap of fun. Anyway, she sent me the season's greetings and twenty dollars, which was a fortune. You can buy a lot of coffee with twenty dollars even now. Gay asked me to come home with her.

At first I thought I wouldn't because I thought that she was patronizing me and besides, she had a most elegant hat — a sweeping brown felt with a feather —

with which I could not possibly compete. Also, she asked me with reluctance. I may not have been the brightest person on the third floor, but I knew reluctance when I saw it.

However, Len said, "What in the name of God will you do here?"

Well, I knew what I would do. My aunt had also sent a box of cupcakes, and I would brood and munch them.

So all three of us went down to Boston together.

The first part of the trip was fun. No matter how Joe-College you didn't want to be, there was a certain pleasant hysteria about that train. It picked up students all along the line, some of them wearing porkpie hats and many of them trying to press against you in the vestibule. And how they sang! And how they pretended to be tiddly! There was a sort of nontruth going: we were collegiate and so there were no holds barred and everybody loved us. Or at least put up with us. At one end of our car a lusty group of males sang "Violets" and at the other the girls vied with a real dandy, which I sort of like even today:

> Oh father, take the cow away
> Take her out of sight . . .

As more of the impossible young got on at Bates and Bowdoin the conductor got more dour and the three of us more self-conscious. I don't know why we thought we had to prove something to the conductor, but I think that is what we were trying to do. While the girls combed out their heavy waves and the boys tried hard to look drunk, we drew apart.

> *For I am heavy-hearted*
> *And I cannot milk tonight . . .*

What do you suppose was the matter with us that we couldn't mill up and down the aisle? I don't know — we felt different.

There used to be an hour's wait in Portland before you made connection with the Boston train, and that was the wait that separated the sheep from the goats, because the provincials got off there and their mothers met them. After that Len got very quiet.

After that Gay fell asleep.

There was something touching and vulnerable about her profile, caught on the train window. The elegant hat was just a little askew. Under the haughty brim her light hair was tumbled, and every time the train jerked on the tracks the pheasant feather brushed against the glass.

"Is she all right?" Len asked.

"She's all right," I said. "She just can't milk tonight."

There wasn't anything the matter with her except that she had been sitting up late nights; long after I grumbled and punched the pillow her light was on, and would be on much later when I awoke. Even if she had folded over them, her pages were piled evenly and her reference cards, with their small legible handwriting, were neatly stacked.

There wasn't anything the matter with her except

that she couldn't bear not to be the very best. But she did look white and frail and very beautiful (with the glossy feather bent against the glass) and she slept like a child.

The train went bumpety-bump upon the tracks.

Len had a pint in his coat pocket. "Ooh," I said. "What a nice idea!"

So until we reached Massachusetts and the next contingent got on at the Normal School we nipped at it and laughed (gently) at the conductor, who came around fussing and muttered, "Sometimes there's no sense trying to keep a car looking nice." And then we were quiet for a while. For a girl with light hair, Gay had the darkest lashes.

Len said, "Do you understand her?"

Then all those embryonic teachers got on and the singing started up again — even the same song, by cracky! By that time we had finished the pint and pitched right in with them.

> *For it isn't fair to this here cow*
> *That I should have to milk her now . . .*

And Gay woke up and smiled at us both.

North Station smelled of coal smoke. In those days you couldn't walk through North Station without feeling as if you had a heavy chest cold. It was eleven o'clock. The lights in the train were thin and yellow and we jockeyed for places in the aisle as if it weren't a terminal and if you didn't look sharp you would be carried on past your destination.

Len got our bags off. He asked, as if it were something we had been disputing, "So shall I call?"

Someone caught me from behind with a suitcase, right below the knee. Gay had charged ahead toward the subway.

"Sure," I said. "Why not?"

There were two girls who went on to New York.

5

A LOT OF THINGS were easier to understand once one had seen that house.

It was pushing twelve when we reached Harvard Square and we walked from the subway. Cambridge is nice on a spring night. The movie theater was closed and the windows of the Coop blind. The streetlights had that late lonely look and a solitary cop lounged at the door of the kiosk, taking a gander at the morning papers. A few students wandered by twos and threes, and a lone bicyclist wheeled silently by. The air smelled of April.

Gay said, "Want a cab?"

I didn't want a cab. The night air was fresh and our suitcases light; as soon as we left the pallor of the Square for the dark intricacy of the little crooked streets I took my shoes off. They were spectator pumps with snub toes and they hurt. Everywhere, trees buckled the sidewalks with their twisted roots. We turned left and right and right again, and there was Rackety-Packety House.

It was ablaze, all three storys, and filled with uncles. Actually, only three of them were home, but it seemed like more. They were all young, they were all handsome in a blond, attenuated way. And they weren't old enough.

All in all, there were eight of them; Gay's father had been the firstborn. Gay was the only female in the family. Myself, I would have loved it, but she felt engulfed, as if she had to struggle to maintain a small island of order in a high sea of masculinity.

She opened the front door, tripped over a hockey stick and sighed. I never knew that house to be locked and it wasn't locked that night. On the broad porch there was a temporary little hut to protect the front door from the winter's ravages (Gay said the last two years no one had got around to taking it down); this was filled with cartons from which skates, mufflers and boots overflowed. Everything in that house overflowed. There were too many books for the bookcases, too many coats for the coatrack, too many dishes for the black soapstone sink. Too many uncles. The whole house smelled of cigars.

One of the uncles was making toast, one was washing socks, one (for some reason) was pacing the dining room reciting Latin verbs. They were enchanted to see Gay. She greeted them patiently but without enthusiasm. The youngest was almost young enough to be her brother. I fell in love with all of them on sight, especially the middle one, who left his socks to press upon us cups of villainous coffee; as many times as I was in that house I never saw that encrusted pot off the stove and never saw it washed.

That house — that wonderful house. I couldn't understand my friend, who pulled her gloves slowly from her hands and looked around as if to find a clean place to put them, and then folded them and put them carefully in her purse. She smiled distantly, the way she smiled at freshmen on our floor. She was nice as could be and refused everything; she would have no Whoopee-Pie, no canned milk in her coffee, would take no time to listen to new records on the old phonograph.

"My friend's tired out," Gay said.

Well, yes, I was tired — not that tired. I would happily have seen dawn in through those dusty windows just to keep talking to the three avid, affectionate uncles (one of them had already shown me a snapshot of his girl) and I couldn't understand why she didn't like them. But I hadn't met her grandmother yet, who didn't like them either.

I woke that Sunday morning and lay late (they were all Unitarians, so no one had to go to church), while beside me Gay slept quietly and neatly. There were two other bedrooms up on the third floor, and during the night I had been aware of uncles coming and going; there had been a smell of cigarette smoke and shirts, and the water had kept gurgling in the water tank. It was certainly different from my aunt's place in Waltham.

My aunt taught history and Problems of American Democracy (you may be sure that kept her on her toes) and her small house in an aging development was as confined and tidy as her purse. What used to be my room was now a den and any time that I stayed overnight I slept in a folding bed. Beside that bed there was a gleaming table upon which, always, there was a clean ashtray and a bowl filled with everlasting.

How to describe Gay's grandparents' house!

Gay's room had once been the maid's room, but her grandmother had given maids up long ago. They cost too much, required to be directed, and were always there. Now that the boys were grown they could heat something up for themselves, and when there were no more clean dishes someone would probably wash them. The three flights of stairs were convenient because you could put things on them, particularly the enclosed back-stairs that the maid was supposed to use (when there was a maid) — you could throw the linen down there. The first time I opened that door, by mistake, I found a mound of soiled sheets and a small artificial Christmas tree, still covered with dusty baubles. And a dustpan and curiously enough, a complete set of Dickens. Also a hot-water bottle filled with cold water and tottering stacks of old newspapers from which Gay's grandmother meant, someday, to clip arresting items. The family worried about that stairway because, they said, it was a firetrap, and Gay told me that there was indeed once a fire, but the grandmother wouldn't let anyone call the fire department because she didn't want them to see what a firetrap it was. Somebody put it out.

The kitchen was large and everything in it was either bent or broken. At some point someone had almost put curtains up — every window had rods and from one a limp panel dangled. But who would want to shut out the

tassels of the linden tree? There were two pantries, one
for staples and one for dishes; their condition beggars
description. In the back hall a battered icebox wept.
One of the boys (I was to find) was supposed to empty
the pan that caught the overflow from the melting ice,
but none of the boys ever remembered it and the grandmother never remembered which boy was supposed to
remember. In one of the windows that fronted the street
there leaned a square of cardboard upon which was
printed ten pounds, twenty-five, fifty. You were supposed to turn it to indicate your requirements. Nobody
ever turned it, so the iceman always brought fifty. It was
just as well, because icemen were getting hard to come
by, and no one wanted to discourage this one.

There were books everywhere. They were piled on
the floor and used for paperweights or to hold up uneven
table-legs. They lay open upon the kitchen shelves and
all the chairs, and if it became necessary to close them,
whoever closed them played fair and marked the place
with some sort of bookmark, a whisk broom or a spoon.
Their spines were broken and their covers looked as if
mice had been at them, but every one of them bore the
grandmother's name in her fine Spencerian hand: Mary
Elizabeth Hutchens — and Mary Elizabeth knew where
every one of them was. If you were looking for Vasari's
Lives of the Painters, it was under the radiator in the
dining room. Ruskin's *Stones of Venice* had been in the
bathroom for some time although, properly speaking,
one was not supposed to read in the bathroom. On a
cardboard from one of the grandfather's immaculate

shirts, Gay's grandmother had made that plain. *This is not a library*, she had printed. In Latin.

That first morning, when Gay took me down to meet her grandmother I was a little intimidated because I was about to meet a *savant*, a bluestocking. She sat behind the large Webster's Unabridged, and she looked up and smiled — strictly at Gay. To me, she inclined her head.

Then she said, "Isn't this interesting? I looked up nightingale, and that led right to nightjar and nightmare. Do you know what a nightjar is?" And then with a gesture which was to become familiar, she crossed her arms upon her bosom and rubbed her shoulders back and forth across the back of her chair.

"Did it ever occur to you," she demanded, "that Mood, spelled backward, is Doom?"

Gay's grandmother was a formidable woman, but you didn't see it right away because she was pretty. She was a round little person with a wealth of that good hair that silvers with no trace of yellow; it was puffed over her forehead and coiled in a gleaming knot on top. She wore a cotton housedress (Good Lord, what has become of the cotton housedress?) and high-laced black shoes. Her eyes were very bright.

If she is older than I am, that kind of female scares me. I felt limp and lank, and I knew my nose was shining and my stockings loose.

But Gay said, "Grandmother, this is my friend. This year she won the poetry prize."

And that made all the difference.

I had won the prize, too, and went on winning it, which was the best thing that ever happened to me because it made people take me seriously and kept me from doing so. Lots of young people wish to become writers; there is a kind of person who intends to be a screen star, too. However, once you are in print, people regard you warily. You just might make it, and perhaps at their expense.

But I knew that my poems were awful. I think the judges must have been bewildered by the variety of my rhymes; I expect judges get pretty tired of *vers libre*. I liked the prize money, but senior year declined to be class poet, thus making room for a stern young man whose contribution was economically entitled "Ode." I had decided to rest on my laurels and — except for once — I have been resting on them ever since.

As it turned out, the grandmother was a rampant feminist who rejoiced in any female victory. It wasn't really that Grandmother didn't like the uncles; but she saw all men as dolts. In spite of all her sons — perhaps because of them — she was not much in favor of sexual congress. It was untidy and had dire results and took a lady's mind off more important things.

Like sonnets. So we became friends and spoke about the sonnet.

"With this key," Grandmother said, "Shakespeare unlocked his heart." She rubbed her shoulders.

I felt like saying "He sure did," but I thought I wouldn't.

Instead, I said "A sonnet is a moment's monument."

Grandmother triumphed. "I would rather build a fine sonnet than have built St. Paul's!"

"All right, you two," Gay said.

When Mary Elizabeth was nineteen she was lovely — I've seen her sepia-colored photograph. She didn't go to college because ladies didn't, but in spite of the opposition of her father she did go to a Female Academy. And then she took her skill and her ambition halfway across the country and taught for two years in Muskegon, Michigan, of all places. She said afternoons, after school, they used to skate in the long cold light. Then she came home and married Hobart Hutchens because he was so persistent. And after that it was all downhill.

That's why she was afraid for Gay.

After eight men tugging at her (nine, if you include her husband), demanding milk and clean underwear and leaving their socks and their tobacco everywhere, there was a girl child: clean, smart, and stern. A girl who when she was three understood parallel lines. Who knew her tables at four. And at five could recite:

> Trust thyself. Every heart vibrates
> to that iron chord . . .

Later, the uncle that I liked the best told me something that shocked me. As soon as they were old enough to date, this totally superior mother warned them against kissing. She called it swopping spit.

But that morning, in that wild wonderful library, I felt that I had met my Leader. She was enthroned at one of those handsome desks that are banked with drawers on both sides, and the desk was completely organized: reference books, dictionary, pencils (precisely sharpened), inkwell (do you remember inkwells?), erasers, library paste. Nothing else in the room was organized. Everything else was in a comfortable confusion: out-of-date magazines, ancient copies of the Boston *Transcript*, pencil shavings, old cups of old tea. On the walls a triptych of Simone Martini jostled a photograph of the Old North Church, a large engraving of Dürer's *Death and the Knight* and multitudinous prints (Landseer, Alma-Tadema, Raphael) all put up with pushpins, along with last year's calendar and a laundry list. Gay told me that once she had asked for a piece of paper and her grandmother said, "Well, just bend over and pick one up." I couldn't have felt more at home.

But then something happened. The phone rang and my honest friend lied about it.

It was Len. I knew that it was Len because he had said he would call at nine and by the black marble clock beside the plaster bust of a sardonic Dante, it was nine o'clock. That was a great house for busts: Beethoven in the living room, Schubert in the hall. George Washington in the den upstairs, oversized and somewhat blunted, because Gay had put it in the bathtub once, not understanding that you can't wash plaster.

Anyway, the phone rang. Gay's eyes flew to mine. Then she got up to answer it.

It wasn't always easy at Bellevue Avenue to find the phone, which stood — theoretically — on the hall table under one of those big mirrors that are fringed with hooks to hang hats on. In practice, whoever had used it last often left the phone underneath the table in a welter of overshoes or buried in a detritus of coats and stale sweaters.

Gay spoke briefly, while her grandmother was silent and alert. And then Gay let me down, which is about the only time she ever did.

"It's for you," she said.

I don't know whether the grandmother was fooled; we didn't go into it. Because when I had confirmed that we would meet in the Square at noon of the next day, there were already feet picking down the stairs. You had to pick down the stairs because of the objects on every one of them. Grandmother said, "No one is to go up without carrying something." She also said, "A place for everything and everything in its place." There was always a broom on the first landing, too. No one was to come down without sweeping.

We probably would have been sharply questioned if it hadn't been for those tentative feet. As it was, the grandmother sighed. "Here comes your grandfather," she said.

And as if she spoke of some bestial and unnatural appetite, she added, "He'll want to eat again."

6

WE HAD TO MAKE IT the next day because of a real call
I had received. From my aunt.

"You're not supposed to be around," I said, aggrieved.

"I changed my plans," she said. "I want to see you."

She sounded guilty and excited. Now what? I thought.

"All right," I told her, though reluctantly. "I'll come
out any day this week."

But no, it had to be that very day and over-town. "I'll
meet you at the lunchroom at the Fine Arts." And she
added mysteriously, "Some one will join us." It sounded
for all the world like an assignation: the principal of her
school? The rector of the Episcopal church? Highly
unlikely. And in that case, surely, she would not wish
my witness?

"Half a mo," I said.

Gay and I conferred quickly. Like a proper guest, I
urged her to go ahead with any pleasant plans that should
arise, and to give no thought to my own bitter disappointment. She was flatteringly unwilling to do this.
It wouldn't, she said, be as much fun without me; any-

way, Len had planned to bring a friend and the thought of three together all the day was gruesome.

"And you might have to go back with her and spend the night?"

I might. After all, she was all the family I had, and kind to me always in her robust way. "I might," I said. Well, there you were.

"We'll put Len off until tomorrow," Gay said. She looked both disappointed and relieved.

I ambled along to the Square, concerned about my aunt's change of plan, which might curtail my liberty more than I wished it to be curtailed, and plunged into the concrete bowels of the earth. At Central Square we were joined by the proletariat. Just before the Charles Street station the train rushes through a tunnel, and as far as I'm concerned it can't rush fast enough. Then there's a bad moment when the train surfaces and hurls at the high corners of tenements and you think this time it's really going to jump the track.

I changed at Park Street, which is always cold and drafty, and when we came up on Huntington it was raining. The tracks gleamed silver and in front of the Museum the poor old Indian was getting it straight in the face and the water ran from his bronze-green moccasins that dangle on both sides of that discouraged horse. Inside, umbrellas steamed.

My aunt was sitting alone with tea in front of her and a wrong-colored hat riding her heavy hair at an unlikely angle. As usual, when I saw her I was filled with love and panic and wanted to turn and bolt before I was undone. I've since decided most young people feel this way about older people whom they revere and to whom they owe more than they wish to repay. I suppose even Charley feels like that.

She greeted me warmly but absently and without the usual barrage of questions about school. Not having been to what she called a real college, she was always wistful about banners and coonskin coats and liked to quote Dorothy Parker to the effect that if all the girls at the Yale Prom were laid end to end she wouldn't be surprised. So I've been known to jazz things up quite a bit and offer her stories about football and fraternities we wouldn't have been caught dead knowing about. My aunt would beam and suggest archly that we were all a bunch of little rogues.

That day she wasn't a bit interested; her eyes kept slipping past mine to the door. I invented an acquaintance who had been expelled for stealing the dean's sherry.

"That's nice, dear," she said, patting my hand. Her eyes slipped again.

"There he is," she said. "There's Raymond."

At once a lot of things became clear.

My aunt was both shy and gregarious, which is not a happy combination. She would have liked a lot more friends than she had. I think she was too rowdy to please the maiden ladies, and she had little in common with the wedded ones. So all that year I had been pleased when the name "Ray" kept cropping up, and pictured someone suitable in size and sex with whom she was enjoying a sudden flurry of concerts, theaters and flower shows.

I suppose I should have guessed. But while she was reasonably interested in her students, she had never been one to have personal pets.

Ray was a little boy on the verge of being chubby, the kind who in a few years would watch his weight. He was extremely attractive in an unimportant way. The rosy mouth was never going to show much strength, but the blue boy-eyes were very intelligent. And very sharp, I was going to add, but that would tell more about me than it would about Ray. I don't know, you see — perhaps he was fond of my aunt. His manner to her could not be faulted — it was just short of worshipful.

She certainly was very fond of him. She patted him into the seat beside her and said proudly, "The very best senior I've had in thirty years."

He flushed and said, "Oh, now!"

"Ray is a mathematician," she confided, "but well-rounded. Oh, we aren't letting the grass grow under our feet!"

Which explained the concerts and the theater and I suppose, to some extent, the flower shows. And I suppose she liked to be seen with him by people who could not know that he was not her son. I was not as pleased as you might think. One does not like to be cut out, even if one does not want to be caught in. Besides, his attitude to me was more deferential than I felt the years between us warranted.

"But enough of that," my aunt said gaily. "The body first, and then the soul!"

She had the toasted tuna, and we the egg salad. My

aunt at that time was far from elderly, but I was touched to see how on the well-shaped hands she was so proud of, the skin had loosened. On her ring finger she wore a bad big cameo; above it and below the flesh puffed slightly.

When the last crumb was brushed away she said, above her cold tea, "Now to business."

I had wondered.

It seemed that Ray had few resources, which did not surprise me. But it was unthinkable that he should not go on to college.

She said, "You have a scholarship. Now maybe you can help Ray get one."

I looked at her, amazed. She had seen me through each dogged step, the cringing applications, the bitter disappointments. The shameful pleas to local do-good clubs. The sly search for those whose names would make impressive references and who were patient enough to give those references again and again. I reminded her of this.

My aunt put a finger against her nose. "Ah," she said, "but now you know the people there, and you could drop a word or two. It never hurts to have a friend at court."

I was astonished. My aunt was not a worldly person; neither was she naïve. She couldn't seriously think I could influence the scholarship committee. Or could she? I glanced balefully at the boy. His round, fresh face was impassive. Or was that a glint of amusement in the so-blue eyes?

And then I saw that before rhyme or reason it was

vital to her that she be the one to whom he turned. That she bind him to her with hoops of gratitude. Of course I was furious. I didn't know the boy; I didn't know that I would like the boy. One afternoon of my vacation gone because my aunt was fond and notional. Perhaps I was jealous, too.

I said in the cold tone that everyone recognizes that I would see what I could do. That tone means that is the end of that.

My aunt looked at me shrewdly. And then she looked at Ray and her face brightened. "Oh, he'll get to college," she said. "We've got a trick or two up our sleeve!"

Either the friends with whom she had not shared her holiday did not exist or else she had forgone that holiday (and who knows how much else?) in order to keep that trick up her sleeve. I was wild with pity. How long did she think she could keep that urchin trailing at her skirts?

The waitress brought the check and my aunt deftly scooped it up. "We're going to do American primitives," she said. "Love to have you along."

I wouldn't stay. But I'm glad to say I hugged her warmly, and I'm glad to say I shook hands with Ray and gave him my best smile.

"See you around," I said.

I watched them vanish down the corridor. My aunt barged confidently and the boy glowed at her with love and trust.

Who knows? Maybe he felt that way.

I never did know what became of him, but I suppose

good things. He probably made his name as a statistician or an actuary. Once, years later, I asked my aunt about him.

"What boy?" she said. "I've known so many boys."

She was a proud and lonely person, was my aunt.

7

GAY'S GRANDFATHER was a gentle, lonely person.

Unfortunately, he was flawed from everyone's point of view. He had an office in Central Square but whatever he did there, he didn't do very well, though he had a lot of friends who kept dropping in to help him do it. He was not encouraged to bring those friends home. The fact is that financially, he had erred. Their charge accounts were honored; Gay's grandmother ordered the groceries from S. S. Pierce and his cigars came from Leavitt's. But they were always cutting corners. The grandmother didn't like the way that he bought Western novels when, if he *had* to read Western novels, he could have got them from the lending library, nor the fact that punctually as the sun set, he expected dinner. The boys (except when they needed pocket money or a loan) objected to the fact that he presided over a dwindling income.

And nobody liked the way he drank. Having met the grandmother, I understood Gay's passion for order; after I met the grandfather, I understood her passion for temperance. It was not that he indulged often but when he did, he applied himself to it with fervid, though quiet, enthusiasm. He would go weeks, even months, without so much as a glass of wine, but then — watch out. Of course I didn't know that on the first morning when I heard his feet come pickety down the stairs. He was a handsome man in an anemic way, but rather shy. Grandmother was the one who had the fiber. All through breakfast (we ate in the dining room and help or no help we had huge linen napkins and dented sterling napkin rings) my mind was drawn to a disturbing thought — those eight sons had to come from somewhere, and I kept wondering what kind of satyr he turned into once the bedroom door was closed. Or had turned into. In those days we were pretty sure sex stopped at about thirty-five.

I assumed that she had put up with such indignities because they were what women had to put up with. It didn't occur to me — not then — that a strong woman, even if small, could discourage a shy man any time she wanted to.

There is so much I didn't know at seventeen, just as there is so much that Charley doesn't know even now. I thought people were the way they seemed to be. I really did.

After breakfast, Gay and I washed the dishes. The uncles had come and gone — one was in law school, one worked in the post office; one sold stoves to restaurants. They used a lot of cups. That black soapstone sink was horrid. Slime collected in the corners and the grandmother had a frugal but unpleasant theory about soap.

She had a curious utensil about the size of a matchbox if you can imagine a matchbox made of wire, and in this she kept odds and ends of used soap. You were to agitate this wildly under the faucet and get suds. But the odds and ends of soap weren't proper dish-soap. My aunt, whatever her shortcomings, used Lux in the kitchen and Fels Naptha. The bits of soap with which we tried to remove egg were all too obviously left over after baths.

Gay has a beautiful mouth, but it can narrow. That morning while she scrubbed, it was very narrow. I was pretty sure it had something to do with Len, and indeed it did. When she had squeezed out the dishmop (it was a veritable tiny mop with grey slimy strings) she said to me, "Will you go see if they're through in there?"

I didn't, that first morning, see the pattern but later I knew the pattern was always the same; after breakfast the grandmother tried to get him to sign checks. Mr. Hutchens didn't like to have anything to do with money — probably because it got away from him so easily — and he resisted signing checks. So when it was about time for the credit to be cut off, what she did was to write out the checks herself. Then she said to him, "Mr. Hutchens. Sign."

He owed not only for the cigars and the groceries but for the haberdashers'; he was a classy dresser. And if you charge your brandy, that mounts up. The grandmother never charged anything herself, except at Lauriat's Bookstore, and she never took a chance on that one but paid it herself, out of what she saved on the laundry money.

So I took some plates into the pantry and eavesdropped. I heard the scratch of a pen and observed that on the counter there was a copy of *Tristram Shandy*, lightly dusted with flour. Then I heard Mr. Hutchens rise.

"There, Mrs. Hutchens," he said. "Will that content you?"

And then the chauffeur came. Somehow or other he always managed a chauffeur and a rather handsome car. That year it was a Cadillac with a bud vase. Part of the chauffeur's job was to keep the bud vase freshly filled. Gay said the chauffeur was because Mr. Hutchens was afraid to drive, presumably because he never knew when he was going to drink. Everyone else knew. First, Gay said, he got irritable. The grandmother, rubbing her shoulders against the back of her chair, would say, "The terrible wrath of the male creature permeated the atmosphere." I never did track that quotation down.

Then bottles started showing up in unlikely places: the laundry hamper, the flour bin — grandmother didn't use much flour. In that house, a bottle was never openly displayed.

And then, for unpredictable lengths of time, he vanished into their bedroom. There was never a voice raised nor an ugly scene, only a very high level of tension and utter silence while the taxis came and went and all telephone calls were countermanded. "Mr. Hutchens is suffering from the flu."

Eventually, like a bear out of hibernation, he would lumber forth.

Later that week, I beheld one of these appearances. Gay and I were headed for the brown bathroom with our curlers in hand when we encountered the grandfather, immaculate in a pressed suit from the best tailor, smelling of Aqua Viva, sick, shaking and ashamed. Although myself, I thought he was overreacting. He hadn't been out of it all that long, at least not this time. Maybe it was the burden of old disasters.

Gay pressed her lips together, and I was afraid she was going to say something cutting. I should have known better. She put her arms around him.

"I love you, dear," she said.

"Thank you, little girl," he said. And to my horror, his eyes welled with tears.

Isn't it *hard*. Beyond those superbly tailored, slightly shrunken shoulders I saw, through the open door, the pell-mell and melée of the room in which all those sons had been conceived. His laundered shirts (very fussy he was about his shirts) were stacked on the floor in sliding piles. The bed looked like a bird's nest, and everywhere, *everywhere* was the grandmother's clutter. Open drawers, open magazines. The ubiquitous teacups. Used towels. Dust kitties. From the fireplace (it could have been a very grand room) ashes blew, and grey curtains, laced by sun and time, faltered at the windows.

I wondered how much of her disorder was a cultivated revenge, and how much of his drinking (since most men do not beat women) was a frustrated counterattack. Because their styles were irremediably opposed. And yet, I thought with awe, upon that battleground of a bedroom they had cavorted and the living proof existed. Oh, what nymphs and fauns!

I missed the whole point; I was taken in by their disguises. They loved each other very much and eventually, they died within weeks of one another.

That's something else I wish I had told Charley: there is more going on than you know.

"Grandmother," Gay said. "We have a friend. Well, not so much *my* friend." And no cock crew. "May our friend spend the night?"

Mrs. Hutchens sighed. She folded her arms and rocked slightly. She said, "Wherever will you put her?"

Gay said, "He can sleep in Grandpa's den."

We met at a little bar on Massachusetts Avenue and just for the hell of it went to the Peabody Museum to see the glass flowers. And then we took the subway overtown and spent the afternoon wandering and then we had hotdogs and then we stayed a bit too long at the Merry-Go-Round Bar at the Copley Plaza. Coming back, we had to walk from the Square because the last streetcar had left; it was cold and damp and beautiful and beside the Botanical Gardens (the gates were locked, we couldn't get in) Gay and Len stopped underneath a streetlamp and the mist veiled them like tiny polka-dots, but not so much that I couldn't see the way her gold head dropped and how she strained upward to him.

Oh yes, I had a date, but he had headed toward Porter Square and I forget who he was. All day we had only called him "Hump."

Gay and I were very quiet in the bathroom, which was all marble and brown wood and where from an overhead tank a chain dangled with a handle like some rich wooden fruit. At the foot of the stairs to the third floor the three of us paused before we separated and I could see Gay listening. The uncles were all asleep.

And Gay said, "Would you mind?"

So I was the one who slept in Grandpa's den.

8

I HADN'T SLEPT very much. Even with the window
open, the air in the den was vile with old tobacco smoke.
I have never liked cigars. Besides the lumpy sofa where
I tossed, the room held a large table suitable for confer-
ences, and at the head of it there was a huge black
leather chair in which the grandfather was wont to spend
his time playing a complicated kind of solitaire. There
was also a vast rolltop desk filled, I am sure, with old
secrets which nobody ever plumbed. The grandmother
never moved from the library. The uncles congregated
in the kitchen. Nobody ever seemed to violate the soiled
sanctity of the den.

But I was desperately afraid that that one night somebody was going to blunder in and discover the wrong
person. To prevent this I tried to sleep with my head
underneath the old velour dun-colored drapery that Gay
had found in lieu of a proper blanket. Surely no one
would go so far as to rip the curtain from my head
unless, say, the house was on fire, in which case it would
be every man for himself and the devil take Gay and

Len. But even the levels of stale smoke were better than no air at all and I kept fitfully waking up to find that I had hurled my cover aside and was all too obviously revealed as myself. I was relieved when at last Len's fingers rattled gently on the door.

And mad. After all, nobody likes to lose a lover — and, technically, he was my lover first. "I hope to God you know what you're doing," I whispered at him, and fled for the safety of the bathroom. I didn't really feel at ease until I had pulled the chain to indicate my honest presence there; guests may go to the bathroom at any hour.

I had put on the light first thing because of something Gay had told me once; surely something that would never happen twice. But just the same . . . There were often so many people in that house — uncles, friends of uncles, sometimes the wives of the older ones and their children. Gay, in a hurry, had rushed in one night and hadn't bothered with the light. She pulled her nighty up and sat down on someone. I certainly didn't want to do anything like that.

That was the strangest room. It was too big to have been originally meant for a bathroom, and the house was so old that I imagine when it was built people still used commodes — I've never understood when or by whom they got emptied, or for that matter, where. There was a great cracked marble basin housed in wood, a tub that squatted on lionlike claws, a curious center light of engraved opaque glass from which a long brown string dangled, and the watertank which hovered high over what the grandmother called the facilities ("Would you care to use the facilities?") made one nervous, as if it might suddenly tumble down. When you pulled the chain the water gushed and gurgled in all the pipes. All the pipes showed.

In spite of the grandmother's stern admonition, the bathroom was obviously a library. Everyone in that house liked to read; not that they were all scholars; they just liked to read, and there was no corner of that big house that was not littered with literature, as though they were all afraid that they might be caught at any moment without print. The grandfather had his Westerns, the uncles were given to detective tales on the covers of which guns blazed and girls with round thighs cringed. Whenever she saw these the grandmother would sigh heavily and cover them up with the *Christian Science Monitor* or something really sound on nature. She always hoped that the next son who got restless would pick up the *Monitor* instead of the magazine. He never did.

Her own taste was eclectic. One found Schliemann, Chaucer, Thackeray. Goethe on the umbrella stand, the big Shakespeare variorum on the dining-room table because one might need it at any moment. Also the Thornton W. Burgess *Animal Book* and *The Water Babies*. She had a great interest in queens and whenever she tracked down a good one (Elizabeth of Bavaria was a favorite) she would rub her shoulders against her chair.

About the only thing she didn't read with pleasure was contemporary fiction, which she thought decadent. Certainly fiction was getting suggestive but it was not yet very explicit, which was probably why something so old-hat as *Ulysses* packed such a punch and why — very properly, from Grandmother's point of view — the Watch and Ward Society had kept Molly Bloom out of Boston. But authors were implying more and more, and some of the things they implied the grandmother simply didn't believe. It was too silly.

When I think now of what we considered blue! James Branch Cabell, for instance. My aunt had hoarded an old copy of *Jurgen*, which I still think is funny, although I might not if I went back to it. But that was playing around with phallicism and Freud, both of which were very big in my aunt's time; she didn't like, any more than did the grandmother, the way writers were beginning to mention physical parts, even if they didn't yet picture them in action. All this thrusting and plunging hadn't started yet. But my aunt, who considered herself fairly up-to-date, had thrown *The Grapes of Wrath* across the room (having finished it, first) and said that if she met Steinbeck she would chase him with her broom. Gay's grandmother would not have finished it first.

Picture me, then, sneaking into that bathroom like a guilty thing affright and then a little later walking quite boldly forth, since although I had no right to be couched in the den, I had a perfect right to use the facilities. I swept past the den door, started up the stairs and barked my shins on Volumes I and III of Taine's *English Literature*.

My friend was pretending to be asleep and was breathing evenly in a way she couldn't keep up and which would fool no one. Sullen and damaged, I climbed into the sheets Len had lately vacated and lay staring into the dark. Yesterday's bra and briefs glimmered from where I'd flung them, and I was outraged to think that Len had seen them. What unseemly intimacy! But cross as I was, I knew that was ridiculous. I lay there thinking about Gay.

I was afraid for her.

She was — like all of us, I suppose — such a mish-mash of contradictions. She was the dean's darling, fine and pure and idealistic to the point of nonsense, and yet tonight she had acted like a slut. It was all very well for the likes of me — I was the dean's demon and nobody expected very much. The dean had her eye on me and we both knew it; what I had so far gotten away with was because of stealth and slyness and general bad faith. None of that suited Gay. I knew the dean thought I was evil company for her, and I was beginning to think the dean was right.

Gay said in a very small voice, "Are you mad?"

I thought about it. "No," I said, "I'm not mad." And I wasn't. I was scared, and I was scared for her. No one should give himself like that to another being: nothing held back, nothing protected, nothing reserved for a personal and private rainy day. She didn't see loving, as I did, as a mutual give-and-take at the best and subject to change without much notice. To Gay love was *becoming* someone else; alas, that does not happen.

And there were other considerations, less lofty but more practical.

I said, "Suppose an uncle had come wandering in?"

She said indignantly, "They wouldn't!"

They wouldn't, either. The uncles were all prudes.

"Suppose you get caught?"

"I won't," she said. "He took care of that. But what if I did? We want children one day."

Goodbye degree, goodbye graduate school, goodbye doctorate. Goodbye grandmother.

"Besides," she said in a soft voice, "I have to take that chance."

God damn it. "Why?" I asked. "Just tell me why?"

"Oh," she said. "You know."

I did, of course. Because if she didn't, somebody else would. Like me. The fellows never put it that way, of course; if you won't, it merely proves that you don't love them and perhaps that you are frigid (an intolerable accusation) and they are very, very hurt and look around for someone who can really love them.

"That's a tired argument," I said.

Gay has her practical side. "I know," she said. "But that's because it's true."

And then she lifted her arms and they glimmered in the dusk of dawn. And she whispered in a tone that shivered with joy, "*O lente, lente currite noctis equi!*"

Aubades are splendid.

But no matter how you urge them, those horses of the night go charging right along; morning pales the window, and you have to get up again.

9

So THERE WE SAT at the Ritz, a long long time after that first night, and whatever had gone wrong along the way (believe me, something always goes wrong along the way) they were still together. But I suppose a man gets tired of raping his wife, even if tenderly. No, of course I don't mean that literally. It was Gay's whole way of life that Len had to rape, including the standard she had set for him. Doctors and priests and your favorite professors are always disappointed because physically and spiritually and intellectually you don't meet their standards. "Shape up!" they say. But you don't have to live with priests or professors. Somewhere beneath Len's calm and courtesy there was a man who did not wish to be daily exhorted to shape up. I happen to know.

I recognized that look in his eyes: they flickered. He was tired; he was restless. His manners were always exquisite, especially to Gay. It was one thing that had fooled the grandmother, who could not imagine (I suppose) that any young man who was that polite could really wish to do anything so rude as to get a girl into bed. And he was courteous to Gay, though not enough to order when she wanted to eat. Eventually we got around to it, but not until after she had looked at her watch a number of times and had once asked gently, "Do you have to go back to the office?"

No matter how gently you inquire, that question implies "Are you fit to go back to the office?" And that's a question that strikes at a man's self-esteem, suggesting as it does that no matter how dear he is to his wife, he may seem insufficient to his superiors. It also reminds him that he has superiors.

According to Gay, marriage is total surrender. She really thought they were one flesh, and that what offended her should offend him. I gave up long ago telling her not to make that mistake: we are not one. And no matter how much a man loves his family (Len loves his family) he doesn't like to be harassed at lunch. That piece of paper is not a license for harassment. I felt that Len was right on the edge of something and whatever it was, it was more than getting back to the office in acceptable shape. If you have slept with a man and have, even for the moment, felt an affection for him, you sense some things. There is no knowledge like the bitter knowledge of old lovers.

The fact of the matter is that what everyone is looking for is total acceptance and unqualified approval. Some one person in the world who feels that everything you do is right. Not someone who tries to be a good sport while you make the old mistakes.

Gay was trying ever so hard to be a good sport, but

that is a thing at which she has never excelled. When she is really enjoying herself (and that is always about something very wholesome) those long lovely eyes are alight, but when she thinks people are consuming too much alcohol and wasting too much time, nothing flashes but her smile. Well, it depends upon what you consider a waste of time. Wes has a handicapped child he doesn't like to be asked about because there is never going to be an answer. And, of course, I had my own thing too that I wasn't ready to think about. Neither of us was thinking of throwing the battle. We were both just asking for a little time out.

I looked at my friend, so soignée in her thin white wool, and I wished she were a little easier on others. Because however frivolous we looked to her, at that moment Wes and I were having fun. He wasn't thinking about the wife who had packed her bitterness off for the summer to the big empty house in Nahant. And I wasn't thinking about what I was going to have to tell Sam.

It was just about then that Wes said wistfully that it would be great to just keep on going. And why not? We could take another room and all recuperate upstairs for a while and then we could all meet for cocktails and then go on to dinner and then after that . . . Gay said her youngest was at home and she hadn't arranged anything for his dinner. Wes said for Christ's sake, John was seventeen years old.

And Len said ever so casually that he, for one, had to keep right on going.

Gay looked up and their eyes met for an uncomfortable moment.

"There's a publication party," Len said.

Gay said, "You didn't tell me that."

Len shrugged, as if to show that it was of no moment.

Gay said, "And of course Marta will be there?"

"Of course Marta will be there," Len said coldly. "It's part of her job."

Wait a minute, I thought. What's up?

And at that point Gay surprised me. She hadn't touched her last Dubonnet. Now she lifted her glass and drank it. Didn't sip. Drank it.

"Perfect," Wes said. "We'll all go and then we'll go somewhere for dinner."

"As a matter of fact," Len said, "Gay doesn't like to leave the boy alone."

There was a moment of humming silence. The waiter brought our drinks and our unwelcome food.

Gay asked politely, "Who's it for?"

Len said it was for Larry Lawrence and we were all relieved to laugh.

I used to envy Len those publication parties where you got to see some Shelley plain, some very plain indeed. Even if I had given up my own pretensions, I still thought it was exciting to see someone who had written a real book and had it printed and what's more, not at his own expense. I hadn't discovered yet that there are many people who don't write books and are not impressed by those who do. I know better now. There are even those who don't read them. But in those days, like

Mrs. Leo Hunter, I thought it an enviable thing to look upon the face of genius.

We laughed because we all knew about Larry Lawrence, who annually and surely as Christmas, burgeoned with a book. What's more, give or take a few, he always sold ten thousand copies, which made him valuable to the firm, if not wildly exciting. He trafficked in big business and randy secretaries and the country was filled with little old ladies who pretended that they didn't read him. The little old ladies might ask the librarian, "Do you have any *nice* books?" but when they had tucked their Emilie Loring into their shopping bags, the new Larry Lawrence got tucked in, too.

He was never reviewed at all, except perhaps in the Tuscaloosa *Times* — oh, and in *Publishers Weekly*, which always noted neutrally that "Larry Lawrence has done it again." So naturally he was very jealous about his publication parties. For that reason, in spite of rising publication costs, he always got his party. Because ten thousand is nothing to sneeze at, not if it can be depended on. If there is one thing worse than printing ten thousand copies and selling five, it is printing ten thousand and selling fourteen. New printings are expensive and by the time the books are available the orders are canceled because everyone is reading something else. Larry Lawrence never had a best seller but he never got remaindered, either. So he could count on his cocktails and caviar. Naturally, not Beluga.

Wes said, "Well, can't we come along?"

There were many reasons why not, and Len produced

them all while Wes refuted them. The seventeen-year-old expected his mother home; he could be reached on the telephone. He was extremely intelligent but had never cooked — why should he? — and if Gay wasn't there he would probably just heat a can of beans; what was wrong with that? But she never stayed away unless everything had been arranged in advance and he had a friend in to keep him company. So?

And then Gay said that anyway, she couldn't go to a cocktail party in a suit and Len somewhat surprisingly switched positions and said he couldn't imagine why not.

A very strange thing happens while you lunch. At first, unless they know that you are coming, there is no room at all and the place is crowded with men in business suits who are selling Pan Am and buying A.T.&T. and beyond the windows the world crowds by, intent upon a sale at Jordan Marsh or (since it is May) name tapes for summer camp, or a fix. Speaking of that, why is it that every child knows how to get hold of marijuana? If I wanted some, I wouldn't know where to turn.

But by the time your coffee has arrived, everyone has vanished, and beyond the plate glass no one moves except the old lady who perpetually walks that Aberdeen terrier. The waiter is polite, but no longer chummy. Wes was a little tiddly and needed to go upstairs and have a nap. I didn't think I needed a nap, but in the first half hour after lunch one is never absolutely sure. Len's capacity is legendary, but has been known to fail. Believe you me.

At last Gay looked crisply at her watch (and if you don't think this can be done, you ought to see her do it). "It's only three o'clock," she said. "I need a new dress, anyway."

Fortunately, Bonwit Teller is just around the corner.

10

I should have known how the day was headed when, after the men registered, they started making telephone calls because they didn't know just how they were going to feel later on: This is almost never a good sign. Len and Wes made reservations at Joseph's and at Café Budapest and at Pier One, and then Wes thought of Locke-Ober's, and we all decided that was where we wanted to go, because of the turtle soup.

Then Gay and I watched the men start upstairs. I was outraged (I outrage easily right after lunch) because the bellboy winked at the elevator man. This happens even at the Ritz.

Gay said, "Let's walk. I'd like some air." As usual, her instincts in these matters were perfectly sound.

When we first shopped together, we never dreamed of Bonwit Teller's. Filene's Basement was the ticket. And there is nothing wrong with Filene's Basement, which is filled with treasures that for some reason haven't sold upstairs. Of course you have to do some elbowing. I still remember (the way you do remember something you've been pretty in) a coat I got there that had worked its way all the way down from the French Shop.

A long time later, we went to Bonwit's for the first time and bought hats. Gay bought a broad straw covered with green bows which was reasonable because it was summer and because when the boys were little, she went to church. I bought a black velour with a cock's feather which was not reasonable, because it was not on sale and because the only coat I had to wear it with was tweed. They each cost fifty dollars, which when we first met would have clothed us for a year. And then I had to get shoes, because even I knew you can't wear a big black feathered hat with saddle shoes. Fifty dollars is too much to pay for a hat.

The building Bonwit Teller's is in was once the old Museum of Natural History, an ugly overadorned brownstone that used to have a kind of dowager dignity. Now they have tarted it up with blue-and-white-striped awnings, and I am still unpleasantly surprised to find the perfume counter where the dinosaur used to stand. Gay went straight to the second floor where you find what in lesser stores I have seen called Better Ladies Gowns. Well, Gay is certainly a better lady. She was not surprised when the salesperson greeted her by name. The salesperson did not know my name, but then, I haven't lived in Boston for some time. She did honor my charge account, after the briefest and most tactful absence. I keep several accounts open and scattered around. You never know when you are going to be somewhere else and want a cocktail dress.

Oh yes, I bought one too. It is a silly time to buy a cocktail dress, but I know Sam will understand.

The shoes we found at Bonwit's did not please us, which in itself will tell you something about how we've changed. We should have gone to Joseph Antell, which is right around the corner from the Ritz, but Gay and I like to amble if it is Boston, and afternoon, and May. So we strolled up Boylston Street to Tremont, and there in a little shop we found just what we wanted, and cheap as dirt. Elated, we started back across the Common.

What I've always liked about Boston is that it is so hometown. I'm not talking about the suburbs — nobody knows the suburbs. I'm talking about intown, which is small enough so that at every corner you can recall something that happened to you there, and this is even true about the Fenway.

But it has changed. When Gay and I first started coming over from Cambridge her grandmother disapproved because we didn't wear hats. I wonder what she would think if she could see it now. On the side streets —say anywhere along Filene's or Jordan's, you always had to push your way through the Italians and the Jews and the Southies. They weren't rude, they were just tired middle-aged people intent on getting to where they had to be next, and if they spilled into the streets and crossed where they weren't supposed to cross until the narrow streets were clogged with traffic and the horses of the mounted police danced nervously, it was not because they had anything against the police.

But no one is middle-aged. Or maybe it's just that the young are so conspicuous—nothing divides the generations like the lack of shoes. And on they came, the tall lithe Negro girls with their hair like black dandelions gone to seed and their sullen lovely mouths, the boys black and white with their shirts open to their navels and their dirty toes. And everywhere the couples with their heads bent together and their arms entwined. I liked it. What the hell, it was May.

On a bench on the Common along Tremont Street a young man bent above his girl and played upon her mouth with his as if it were a flute. Nobody noticed. The Hare Krishna group still danced and chanted in their diaphanous gowns. One youngster held a pamphlet to us. It was called *Back to Godhead* and I might have bought it except that Gay, like everybody else, was hurrying by.

"What do they do in the winter time?" I asked.

Gay didn't know.

I wish I'd bought a pamphlet.

We crossed to the Garden beside the rather sinister tunnel that leads down to the fairly new underground parking about which there has been such a scandal, and then on the Garden side we slowed to a saunter. The kites dipped and swirled, the flowering trees foamed, the Swanboats glided beneath the little bridge with the sign that said No Sitting or Standing and where many people sat or stood. We passed beds of pansies, velvet and pussy-faced. We also passed a young man lying on the ground with his head half-buried on his arms and a slime of vomit running from his mouth.

We stopped, startled. "He be all right," a soft voice said. "Just pass on."

God help us, we hurried on.

And then, at the corner of Commonwealth something was happening. There was a cruiser there, with the blue light circling round and round; one moment it stood there alone while the cars backed up behind it on Arlington, and then it was surrounded by marchers, blocks of them, and they turned and trudged past the Ritz, where the flags flew above them. It seemed to me they were younger than the marchers I remembered; more cheerful, more at ease.

"I thought perhaps they'd give this up," I said.

"Habits are at first cobwebs," Gay sort of quoted, "and at last cables."

Why, they didn't look old enough to have habits. And many of them led a real child by the hand. Most of the real children looked as if they were having fun, eyes dancing in their black and amber faces and feet flying. A few were frightened, and hung on to the bigger hand for dear life. There was no band, no singing, just these bright-faced young, silent but friendly while the motorcycles cruised like bees among them, the riders not inimical and not sympathetic; just there. A few people stopped to look; not many. As they passed a fresh and pretty girl broke ranks to offer us a slip of paper.

"Join us!" she said.

I glanced down at the paper. It said

JOHNNY CAN READ

and under that

RICARDO CAN'T!

Gay and I looked at one another. Oh, twenty years ago, by all means; even ten. How could we join them now, two middle-aged women with our purses and our coiffures and our big paper bags from Bonwit's, sprinkled with violets? Nobody joined them, not even the kite-flyer or the flutist. They straggled out and passed; the last motorcycle burred behind them.

Gay said, "Charley is still in Canada."

And then the taxis began to move again.

11

IT HAS ALWAYS BEEN Gay's theory — not a bad one, at that — that twenty minutes in a hot tub does as much for you as a nap. Gay went first and while I listened to the predictable sounds of the water gushing and then gurgling I lay upon the bed and was suddenly bone-tired and cranky, and I wished to hell I had something to read. It is very dangerous to get caught without something to read.

The closest Gay and I ever came to a real quarrel was over books. We used to buy our texts together because neither one of us could afford them all, which was fine until it came time to divide them up. The last days before graduation are bad enough, God knows — out of the womb you go, ready or not. The halls rang with the laughter of the girls who were going to be brides in the next week (and widows shortly after) and Gay and I glared at each other. Who was to have *The White Devil?* Who was to have the collected Blake? And who the eighteenth-century drama? We came to some kind of terms, but years later I had a twinge of resentment when I found *Aureng-Zebe* propping up the broken leg of Charley's crib.

Now that we can buy anything we want we seem to read detective stories.

What I really missed was an encyclopedia; an encyclopedia can always cheer you up. The *Americana* is my choice, eleventh edition, 1928. I'm really not all that interested in what's been going on since 1928, and the eleventh edition is a gold mine for those who, like Autocylus, are snappers-up of unconsidered trifles. Well, for instance, what do you know about Theodore Watts-Dunton, beside the fact that he was Swinburne's pal? Ah, he was more than that. In 1897 he composed and published a poem entitled (and I quote verbatim) "Jubilee Greeting at Spithead to the Men of Greater Britain." I'll bet you didn't know that. I like that Spithead. The thought of it has brightened many a sorry morning.

And without the eleventh edition, I would never have known!

Or take this, which concerns whiskey, a topic in which many of us are interested. Those undesirables which contaminate the product are known in America as the heads and tails. In England they are called feints, which gives one pause. Among these is fusel oil, ". . . from which it is very desirable that the spirit should be freed as much as possible." Any way you want to take it, that statement is correct.

But you can't very well lug an encyclopedia around hotels. Fortunately, I did have my flask.

Gay came out of the bathroom all damp and perfumed

but wearing, of course, the slip that she had worn all day which perhaps explains why she looked a little grim. Gay prefers to have all her underthings very white and very tailored while I, who am too big for it, prefer a riot of ruffles. There was a brief bad time when I became one of those women who take a voluptuous gown and peignoir everywhere they go and always always end up sleeping in their slips. That's over now. But it is one reason why I didn't mention the flask to Gay, at least not then.

It is another part of Gay's theory that after the bath you recline in silence with your feet up. So, she on her bed and I on mine, we lay silently, and I cannot guarantee what she was thinking about, but I was thinking about feet, which show the passage of time. Nails thicken and turn yellow, joints swell and redden. Hairs appear on the great toes. I suppose you could shave them, but I am not going to do it. I used to have very pretty feet.

I was also thinking that I must get up and run more water in the tub (which Gay would have left gleaming) because only a real slattern would put on a new dress without a tub, and yet at the moment it seemed an impossible effort — all that doffing and donning. On the seat of one of the armchairs my balloon lay, pink, shrunken and suggestively shriveled, and over the back my new dress spilled with the price tag dangling. Ah — all the prices we have paid! And for a treacherous moment I wished my friend were home in Cambridge. In which case I might not go out to dinner at all.

Then the phone rang.

Gay reached for it without opening her eyes. "It's Sam," she mouthed. That was just habit. We don't expose each other without query and consent.

And I was suddenly undone. I shook my head.

So Gay said lightly and reliably, "She just stepped out, Sam. Shall I have her call you back?"

She put the receiver down and didn't ask. I don't suppose I had to say anything but I did, because there was a certain perverse comfort in it.

"It's just that I can't talk to him," I said.

Her silence chided me. Gay really doesn't know Sam very well, but she likes the idea of him. She thinks he keeps me safe and relatively happy. And if he could, he would. You can't blame Sam for what is happening to me.

Lately I have been trying to remember all my good aunt's advice, although it doesn't really seem to help. Live, she said, so that you can meet your God. She also said, never go out without your underpants in case you should have an accident. Believe me, that was sound advice. And she told me that I had a good angel and a bad one, which used to scare the hell out of me at night.

They don't scare me any more, but I still hear them once in a while. Like yesterday. One of them said, "You're not doing right by Sam."

"Why not?" I answered. "He's just peripheral, a Johnny-Come-Lately we took up with out of loneliness and itch."

And then the one says, "How fair do you think that was?" And the other shrugs and says "Oh — *fair*."

"He has been faithful to you." Yes, but I didn't ask

him to be faithful. Anyway, I've always thought he wedded just to be bedded comfortably and without all that seize and search.

"He is kind."

"Yes, he is kind."

"He loves you. Maybe not like a daemon lover — and why in the world do you all keep whining for your old daemon lovers? Yours is probably fat now and wears one of those pneumatic belts that melt it off while he counts his stocks."

"No. He is dead."

"Well, lucky you. Forever will he plead and you be fair. And by the way, is this bitchery because you're jealous of Sam's first wife? You can tell me; I'm your best friend."

"Well, maybe."

"I thought as much. Why don't you give the man a ring and let him know what's up? He is your legal mate."

"Look — I intend to. I'll call in the next half hour; in all probability. Meantime, shut up!"

They shut up.

12

AT FIRST I said I thought I wouldn't.

That was when Sam first wanted me to marry him, a step that seemed to me unnecessary if not irrevocable. He put his big hand over my big hand and asked, "Why not?"

Sam is presentable and patient and very attractive if you like the type, and any woman of his is going to be secure in every way. I don't think an unkind thought has ever crossed his mind — or any other kind of thought, I sometimes think. I am not talking about business decisions. When it comes to business decisions Sam is the cat's pajamas. At that time, to tell the truth, he bored me just a bit. He had no opinion at all about the Dead Sea Scrolls. But at that time, also, I was lonely and adrift.

Much as I love Gay and Len, they are only friends. Friends are fine at the beginning of one's life and, I'm hoping, can be some comfort at the end, but during the interim they are about their own business. I think that at the end friends are probably more help than children. No matter how well sons and daughters mean, the fact of the matter is that in the end one is in the way. There are all sorts of things that they must be about and anyway, they don't like to be reminded that they are next in line.

To contradict Mrs. Patrick Campbell, I rather preferred the hurly-burly of the chaise longue to the deep peace of the double bed. Still, I was lonely, and Sam was eligible.

So why not?

It was that damn daemon lover that nobody forgets. Sam was no daemon lover.

I'm glad I don't have a crush on Len anymore and that when I did it was briefly and a long time ago. It wouldn't have served. But I'm still partial to him. They say one has a tendency to keep falling in love with the same type and Barry was the same type, only more so. He had Len's suavity and his discernment, and he had other things. I loved his black hair and his black rages and his epigrams, and I respected his hangovers (anyone would — they were colossal) and I enjoyed our quarrels. Well, they weren't really quarrels. They were *fights*.

It didn't matter then that we didn't have children; they would have been crushed between us, anyway. Just being in his bed sufficed, and I would have done anything, *anything*, to be the one who got to run my hands along his long hard runner's legs and over his hard shoulders. Sometimes when he was gone during the day I used to open the closet door and bury my face in his jackets just for the comfort of it. Then he ran out on me.

He did. He came home one sunny afternoon and told me he was going to. The sunlight, I remember, lay in yellow strips on the Aubusson; the hired boy had mowed the lawn and the house was filled with the fragrance of cut grass. Barry was furious. I forget what the pretext was but I knew it was a pretext because I would never have done anything to make him furious, except on purpose. So I came right out and asked.

He said, "I didn't pass my physical."

I knew that for some time he hadn't been feeling topnotch, but he hadn't told me he was going to see a doctor. "I suppose that's my fault?" I demanded. And then because I was cold to the core with fear I picked up an ashtray — crystal, rather a heavy one — and threw it at him. It gave him a shallow but ugly cut and it gave me the chance to comfort him.

But just the same, he had to go away and after a while, he did.

For a long time I sulked and wept and mumbled Tennyson and Shelley:

My life has crept so long on a wounded wing . . .
I fall upon the thorns of life! I bleed!

It was right along then that I had such trouble, nights, remembering to get out of my slip. And then one day Gay, who had been very understanding but was getting sick of it, reminded me that I've never liked Tennyson much and loathe Shelley.

She was right. So after that, if the fellow and the time were right, I started having an occasional affair,

which is less debilitating than grief and more fun. Not
that I have ever gotten over Barry. Sam doesn't hit me;
I think because that isn't his way of caring. I've never
thrown an ashtray at him, either, though come to think
of it, I did once slap him with a *Harper's*.

So I told Sam, "No. I guess I won't."
But then my aunt began to ail.
I honestly always tried to be attentive to her. Nobody knows better that I that I owed her a great deal;
it couldn't have been easy for her to take her brother's
brat, especially since, although she dealt with children
every day, she didn't really understand them. I think
she might have come to understand them if that first
fellow hadn't got away. And after a while I recognized,
uneasily, that the fact of me may have stood between
her and finding another fellow. Maybe not. My aunt
was jolly and had more opinions than most men like
a woman to have. And teachers have a way of getting
more so; the ones that don't scuttle out of the profession
quickly are likely to stay for a long, long time. Poor
love. She'd always wanted to be the life of the party,
but she was only asked to the party just that once.
Anyway, I remembered her on birthdays and at
Christmas and went to some trouble finding something
she might really like. And I wrote frequently and telephoned her once a month and never, never, came to
Boston without seeing her. But all that doesn't amount
to very much. I wasn't there to giggle with or to complain to or to sympathize when she had a cold or her
stomach was upset or that McPherson boy had been

fresh again. I assumed that her days were filled with committee work and gossip with her colleagues and maybe outings with a close friend or two. I really thought that — until she went into the hospital and it was the principal of her school who wired me. He was as close a connection as she had.

That little house in the development had achieved its own individuality at last. The handkerchief of lawn was ragged and a tree she had planted as a sapling had grown enough to cut the light from one window. All the paint had weathered and begun to peel. I don't think she had given up, I think she had just stopped noticing, the way you don't notice getting older because you see yourself every day. And when the key had grated in the lock, I found that all that order had at last succumbed to an accumulation of artifacts. As she grew older, she began to be comforted by small china dogs and plastic paperweights with colored objects embedded in them and miniature lobster pots that said "Souvenir of Cape Cod." There were a whole lot of things like that.

It was the melancholy hour of a melancholy November day. I turned the thermostat up and listened to the drip of water from a kitchen tap. It was plain that she had expected this trip to the hospital; the kitchen was immaculate although the linoleum was more worn than I remembered, the refrigerator had been defrosted and the plants watered and the dust on the polished furniture was a light, late dust.

It was plain that she expected to come back, too. The papers on her desk were in neat disarray — incoming bills and those marked Paid were sternly controlled by rubber bands but neither had been put away and the cubbyholes were clogged with my old letters. She would not have wanted me to know she kept them. There was also an old copy of *Holiday* with an article about Mexico City, where I had been, briefly, the year before.

The terrible clues that people leave behind them. On the mantel was a conch shell that I had sent her from Antigua. And on the walls in little ten-cent-store frames hung what must have been every snapshot I ever sent her. I wish I had sent more. And the laughing picture of herself in the middy blouse. She had a rather good Hi-Fi and there was still a record on the turntable. I looked at it idly. My merry aunt who liked "Red Sails in the Sunset" and "The Music Goes Round and Round" and "Roll Out the Barrel" had been playing "Sunday Morning Coming Down," which is not a jolly song.

There is something about Sunday makes a fellow feel alone . . .

I went out to the kitchen and foraged for a drink. And found myself wishing passionately that she had had more things: more snapshots if that is what she wanted, a house with an upstairs bedroom and a garden, a better car, a trip to Mexico City. There was no reason why I couldn't have taken her. I passionately wished, too, that I could find a drink. There was nothing on the cupboard shelves and nothing underneath the sink and I had about decided I would have to call a cab when I decided that a single lady of regular habits might not like to leave her bottle where the delivery boy would spot it. So I poked into the closet and sure enough, in a brown purse with a broken strap I found my father's flask.

Yes, there's something about a Sunday ...

I thought about her getting up on a Sunday morning and starting her coffee, a big woman like me but with her shoulders in the old wool bathrobe bent, the way they do when you get older and maybe muttering to herself a bit in a way she had developed lately or writing some little note to herself, which she did, too — "See pg. 87. Good!" A cup of tea at twelve and the six o'clock news and a slug from the flask and Walter Cronkite. And then nothing ahead but Monday morning.

I didn't blame myself. There was no way I could supply what she was missing short of moving in with her and even that wouldn't have done it. Because she just didn't come first with me. There had never been anyone at all to whom she came first.

And so a few days later, there was no one at all to notify except the principal. He said, in the hushed voice with which one receives such news, "I'm very sorry. She would have retired next year, you know. I was going to see if I could get them to dedicate the yearbook to her."

I wish they had.

I stood there by the table that held the telephone and with one finger made idle circles in the dust. Or maybe they were zeros.

Then I called Sam.

13

GAY SAID, "Are you and Sam having trouble?"

"Only in a way," I told her.

No matter what anyone thinks, Sam and I are attached to one another, very much attached. He is kindly and good and so much in love with his first wife that I have never really felt as if we were married, though God knows it is all perfectly legal. Sam is a very legal-minded person and all papers are in order and everything apportioned fairly and squarely down to the last bond. He is a nice man, honest and reasonable and fair. It is true that I never expected to end up with a vice-president.

"Gay," I said, "do you remember Harry Davidson?"

Harry was the best boy in our whole class. Every Recognition Day he was recognized: class president, treasurer of the Foreign Relations Club, secretary of the YMCA and even, oddly, best runner of the mile. He was festooned with good conduct medals. He was also devoted to Gay and intimidated by her, since he knew virtually everything there is to know about genetics and virtually nothing about English literature, which he seemed to consider an exotic subject and just a little dangerous. He was the one boy I knew who never cut chapel and all good things were predicted for him. He died on the beach at Anzio.

We lost a lot of friends in that war.

"Are you saying that Sam is like Harry Davidson?"

Well, not really. Sam is quite a hand in bed and somehow I can't imagine Harry would be — although that isn't fair, because who knows? Harry had little time to woo and wed and I'll bet died a virgin.

That war began before we got to college. Gay and I were fierce pacifists and read the morning papers before breakfast stony with disapproval. That sort of thing was never supposed to happen again. We had been taught to scorn William Randolph Hearst and hoot at the notion of the Yellow Peril and to respect the League of Nations. We couldn't believe the Germans and the English and the French were at it again. Gay's grandmother believed it. She took no sides but she believed all right, because it was just the sort of disorderly way that men behave. "And have," she pointed out, "since the beginning of time."

There was a lot of talk about ROTC because a lot of the fellows thought we were going to get into it, and Len and Gay had a fight because he said if we did, he was going to enlist. Gay cried, but it was because of the fight and not of the war. Then two things happened. One morning the headlines said PARIS FALLS. The city of lights, the home of Shakespeare and Co. The haunt of Joyce. And it was all real — men rolled down those avenues in tanks. There was a picture in *Life* magazine of a middle-aged shabby Frenchman in a beret. He was crying. And then we went to Cambridge for a weekend and Gay's grandfather had buckets of sand in every room to put out flames when the bombs started falling.

All right, we believed in it. We had to. But we did not approve. There was a near riot on the campus when a German exchange student tried to raise a red flag and was prevented. Gay and I raised our brows. Then Dunkirk happened to us all. We listened to the radio all night as the little boats went out to bring the army back. Englishmen. People like us. At least in that war there were a few gallantries. The Dutch hiding Jews. The King of Denmark with his yellow star. The soldiers waiting up to their waists in water for the little sailboats to take them home.

Gay and I followed the news with awe, and my prize poem that year was a sonnet that compared spring to an orchestra (I would not like to explain this now) and that ended ". . . but in a leitmotif there runs/ The dark andante of the distant guns," though what I thought a dark andante could be, I cannot think.

In the next years, the news kept trickling back to us. A boy with whom I had fretted in Biology lab was blown to bits. Harry didn't survive the invasion of Italy. A fellow who was engaged to a friend of ours crashed on a training flight. Another was drowned at Kwajalein. One young man we knew very well indeed broke and leaped from a signal tower.

Such things are sobering. Thinking of them, all these years later, made me restless.

I eased from the bed, in case Gay was asleep — like a cat, she could sleep suddenly and lightly — and went to stand by the window. We had a corner suite. The rooms at the Ritz are much like nice hotel rooms anywhere; it is the service that is special. I like, for instance, the fact that each floor has its own miniature kitchen, prepared at any time to rush you what you want. And I like the way the corridors are patrolled at night. I'm one of those who always rather expects to be burned to death in a hotel fire and besides, in these abandoned days, you're never quite sure what to be afraid of.

The last time Sam and I were in Boston we were uneasy — perhaps because it was not a particularly happy occasion. But we were surrounded on the corner of Arlington and Boylston by a group of young people who were panhandling. They were modish young people by their own peculiar standards and the amount of well-dressed leather they wore and the beads and deep fringe didn't look like poverty or need. And they were working for no cause: it was just that we had money and they wanted it. One of the girls talked and the others circled us silently. It was strange how dangerous it felt, right there in the middle of the city with shoppers passing. When a police car eased by, Sam shouldered through the ring and we walked on. I don't suppose they would have done anything.

No, the rooms are nothing particular, but the view from the Ritz if you are on the Garden side — that's something else. The Garden lay below all green and tapestried with flowering shrubs and trees and the diagonal walks slant off toward the rosy old buildings on Beacon Street and the gold bubble of the State House. Beacon Hill isn't really much of a hill. It rises from the Common to the faded quiet elegance of Louisburg Square and then tumbles down through a block or two of slums to Cambridge Street and that dread bastion of science, the Massachusetts General Hospital. They're clearing those slums now and handsome colorless government buildings are rising on their sites. There won't be much left to Beacon Hill. Well, hidy-ho.

Upon those walks and on the grass tiny figures strolled, just dots of color from this height, like a pointillist painting or a scattering of confetti, but I knew that a lot of them were young. And it gave me a strange feeling to think that those good young men who went to school with us two wars ago, time had arrested. They are as young as these strolling youngsters, and have been lying, quiet, all these years. I wonder what it is like, being dead.

"What's the matter?" Gay asked quietly.

"Nary a thing," I answered. "On with the dance. Let joy be unconfined." And I began to prowl about for my purse and a cigarette; that sort of thinking is profitless and should be interrupted by bright lights and strong drink.

"You smoke too much," Gay said.

I felt better when Gay was awake. There are a woeful lot of people I have wished would not wake again. That's a slimy thing to say but I mean it. I have collided with people that I later wished were dead. Haven't you felt that way? Strangers and hysterics? I meet a lot of them on planes.

Her cool loving voice. "You do, you know. You smoke too much."

Gay never meets anybody wrong on planes.

When I have bad dreams, Gay is often in them. In my bad dreams she tries to hide my drinks, although it has been years since I drank too much, and while she hides them (not very successfully) she tells me Barry won't like whatever I am doing and I resent it bitterly because while Barry was alive I didn't drink too much and what I really resent is simply that he died.

Sam has very bad dreams too.

I know she thinks that Sam and I are quarreling. As long as she has known me I have usually been quarreling, especially when sex is involved, but what she doesn't know isn't going to hurt her. Yet.

To divert us, I asked about the boys.

There is always something to report about the boys, who have been in warm water if not in hot for a good portion of their brief and on the whole becoming lives, being given to perfectly acceptable mischief. Nothing mean or nasty: minor thefts, broken windows, fistfights, disappearances. I always thought that as parents, Len and Gay meant too well. They gave — oh, how they gave! — too much of their time, all of their interest and a disproportionate amount of their money. The boys went to private schools — day schools, of course, since they must be gathered into the nest at night. Evenings, weekends and all vacations belonged to the children first. Len and Gay read aloud, taught them tennis, toured every spot of remotely historical interest, rented (and then bought) a summer place where they could all play football on the lawn during the long pale summer evenings. In return they asked only that the children be completely happy, cooperative and successful. Only that.

Now when I asked for them, that shallow line appeared between Gay's brows. John has a mild enough track record — a few truancies, a few bent fenders, a few inappropriate friends. Right now he has a tendency to mope and shies like a colt at the college boards; he isn't at all sure that he wants college. His headmaster says if he doesn't get on the ball, the question is unlikely to arise.

Ah, but Charley — Balder the bright and beautiful!

Charley never brought home a paper without a gold star and his poems and stories were always on the bulletin board. In the fifth form he won a statewide writing contest and then a National Merit Scholarship and he elected Harvard and was accepted there. That was one side. There was another side. Charley also ran away at eleven and was gone for a week. At sixteen he took Len's Aston Martin and totaled it after a local cop shot a tire out. He was asked out of prep school when they found marijuana in his room and taken back when a friendly court put him on parole. Freshman year, in spite of some odd goings-on, he was president of his class and the first semester of his sophomore year he almost flunked out. He told his startled parents that the only reason he stayed at all was to avoid the draft.

Gay was baffled. Being all of one piece, she couldn't understand his ambiguity. Len, I think, could. Len has become a very sober citizen. But it was not always so.

"Listen," Gay said, and in a trice (what do you suppose that is?) I was out of the past and back in that soft-carpeted, quiet-colored room above the sun-splashed Garden. "Listen . . ." I know that tone from way back. It means she is in dead earnest, and I got ready to thrust and parry and to fall back from one prepared position to another to the last barricade, which I would defend with all my might — just what was the purpose of this trip? Was that what was on her mind?

I needn't have worried. She wasn't thinking about me at all.

Since I saw her last, Gay has picked up a mannerism; she runs her hands through her short curls. She did this now. And speaking too lightly she said, "Let's stay off the subject of Charley tonight. OK?"

"Sure," I said. "Why?"

Once in a while her grin is impish. "Oh, Len's all uptight."

"What's the matter with him?"

"Nothing, except that he's gone to Canada."

I wasn't talking about Charley. "I mean what's wrong with Len?"

Gay fished a piece of ice from the vacuum bottle by her bed and bending over, began to rub her face. She always does this when there's any ice around. She maintains it's why her skin looks young. Maybe so. Then she had to get up for a towel and what she said next was muffled.

She said, "You noticed?"

Naturally I had noticed.

"He's worried about Charley."

It wasn't, she said, that Len was all that gung-ho about the service. He himself had worn the uniform but if I remembered (I did remember) not with his first enthusiasm. But he had accepted the necessity the way that one accepts the weather. The thing that bothered Len was not that Charley was frightened — he wasn't frightened one bit — but that he just wouldn't accept necessity. He didn't like the war: he wouldn't fight it.

"They're odd," Gay said. "They don't worry about the sort of thing we worried about — like eating." That line between her brows was back. "Charley abominates the State. He feels that Big Papa owes him quite a lot, but not that he owes Big Papa anything. He just won't *accept.*"

"Oh, I don't know," I said. "I'll bet he's still accepting checks."

"Don't be cheap," she said.

But she knows I love Charley. "It's our fault anyway," Gay said. "We *taught* him that!"

I know what she had taught him. That even if Christianity had never worked, the Christian ethic was the best thing man had thought up since the cave: it is not natural or necessary to put others down. As if she read my mind (she probably can after all this time) she said, "*Thou shalt not.*"

I'll bet that's not what Len taught him. I'll bet what Len taught him was that the strongest buck in the herd can afford to be gentle. Either way, they are both astonished that he turned out gentle. And that because the fish have always multiplied in the net, he expects them to. It is no miracle to Charley.

In that nice room the light was fading.

"What time's this shindig anyway?" I asked.

"Oh, sevenish."

"I happen to have a flask along," I said. "I don't suppose you'd be interested?"

She surprised me again. "Why not?" she said.

Another good thing about the Ritz is that there are always extra glasses in the bathroom.

Gay and I used to have no modesty and strode around before each other innocent as Eve. We don't now, although it isn't so much modesty as vanity that makes us keep a wrap handy. It is all very well while the flesh is taut on the bones. Gay doesn't want me to see all those satiny childbirth marks and I don't much want to see them. There's a lot I don't want her to see, either. Trailing my ruffles and my machine-made lace, I handed her quite a jolt of Jack Daniels.

"Well," I said, "kindness and bumps. They'll get amnesty anyway," I told her. "After a while."

We touched glasses. "Anyway," she said, "what's wrong with Canada?"

After a few sips Gay lifted her legs and stretched in a lithe way that does not seem fair to me. She said, "So no talk about Charley tonight. OK?" And then she put a narrow ankle out and eased a stocking over it.

I said, "OK."

But there was something more that I had to know.

They say there's no love like a parent's love and I suppose that's true, although there's exasperation mixed up in it too, and most parents I know feel a certain relief when the racket and discipline and the wet bathrooms and constant meals and demands are over and they have the house to themselves again. But you can love a child very much who is not yours at all, especially if you have had a hand in his rearing. I used to stay with Charley once in a while when Len and Gay wanted to get away. That was back before John was thought of.

Anyway, I'm his godmother. I stood there in front of Christ and everyone and renounced for him the devil and the flesh. I had a right to know. "Is Charley with some woman?"

I hoped to God he was.

"I suppose so," she said. "He usually is." She was looking critically into the mirror and smoothing something on her face. "He hasn't said, though, and it's hard to tell these days when they all sort of live together. But Charley's always had somebody."

Only one that was special, though. I don't have many secrets from my friend, but I do have that one bad secret about the girl who was special. I've cared too much for Charley, given him too much, kept too many secrets for him. Mea culpa.

Gay said, "He's a good-looking boy." He is, too. He looks a lot like Len.

Gay had begun to shake very gently, the way she used to do before exams. When that happens she gets active, to disguise it. She whirled around on the stool and her short curls bobbed. There's a new silver streak in the gold that is more attractive than anything my hairdresser has been able to cook up.

She said, "Charley just doesn't want to hurt anyone."

No, he wouldn't want to hurt anyone. Never again.

"If Len is being unreasonable right now it's because Charley's so unpredictable. It worries him."

And well it might.

14

"ARE THEY HAPPY?" Charley once asked me. "I know they love each other. But is my father happy?"

Happy as most, I wanted to say. Meaning, sometimes and sometimes not, like everybody. At seventeen, Charley didn't believe in means and averages. I don't say he didn't approve of them — he didn't believe in them. He believed in Olympian heights and Stygian depths. He didn't know how delicately it is all balanced; that even in grief a shaft of sun can rest upon your shoulder like a hand, or that even true love can harbor true discontent.

He scowled at me. "I asked you a question," he said.

That was his first year at Harvard and he was creating, and I mean many things — poems, scenes, friendships and disasters. Gay and Len happened to be out of town, so I was staying at the Continental, which was a small good hotel just off the Square on a tree-lined street where the traffic is light, the lobby small and dim, the bar small and dark. I had made the mistake of keeping him waiting for half an hour because when he called from the lobby I was still in my bath, and when I got down he was at the bar with a middle-aged and amused couple who had been buying him drinks.

He never got in that shape in half an hour, though.

What he claimed, rather proudly, was that he had been drinking muscatel all afternoon in his room. I always thought it was a mistake to let him live in the Yard.

"No classes today?" I asked.

He dismissed the idea with the wave of a grubby hand. I dismissed the idea of dinner at the hotel. He looked like an apprentice bum. He was wearing a navy pea jacket someone must have discarded, probably in an alley, pants slick with dirt, and heavy leather sandals over thick white socks. I was wild. I am the sort who likes a good dinner adequately served and in the company of someone who will not make others look askance. One of Charley's tenets at that time was that no one ought to be embarrassed and I had honored it; I had not, for instance, suggested that he bring a friend. I pointed this out.

He said I hadn't understood. What he meant was that no one should *feel* embarrassment. Embarrassment wasn't real. Real was a very big word with him that year.

He said, "Are you teed off?"

I said, "I'm fairly well teed off. Besides," I said, "what if somebody saw you?"

He grinned. "They'd be glad it's just liquor."

Meanwhile I had mentally eliminated every decent restaurant and we ended up in a small shabby joint with harsh light eating hamburgers at a bare splintered table and waited on by a sluttish girl whom Charley seemed to know well, because he called her Rosie.

I blew away some old ash Rosie had not removed and was careful not to get my elbows on the table; I was wearing a very nice suit.

By his third hamburger he had sobered up enough so that I was able to say, "Now I'll ask you a question. What have you got against your mother?"

He was startled and looked up, his eyes very blue in his boy's face. "Why, nothing at all. I love my mother."

"Then why this flouting of what she would wish?"

For a while we held speech, not with but against each other. It was a little like speaking Spanish to a Portuguese. I gathered that he thought it was just like Gay (and me) to think that clothing mattered. What mattered was soul. Custom constricts soul and authority constricts it worse. Therefore it was his responsibility to resist all custom and all authority.

"Bullshit," I said, and felt suddenly just like the dean of women.

Charley said the whole university was a laugh. All these preppies and jocks rushing about doing every last thing right so that some day they would find their own little place in the big machine. Where were they at? He could experience more sitting on the fire escape with Rimbaud's *Bateau Ivre*. I had a sneaking sympathy, although I found his example unpleasantly appropriate.

And this, he said, is why he worried about his parents,

who had been subservient to custom their whole lives. It had prevented them from becoming real.

There was obviously no sense in pursuing this. "Walk me back to the hotel," I said. "It'll be good for you."

Charley stumbled along through the November dark and I stumbled along beside him — those pavements are deadly if you have on heels. We passed the place where the elm used to stand under which Washington first took command of the army; when that elm was cut down in the twenties my aunt procured a piece; she was very pleased with it. The cold stars drifted above us like white sand and the last leaves rattled on the trees. Then Charley threw up his head and howled like a coyote and I looked around to see who had heard.

"What was that in favor of?" I asked.

Do you know what he said? He said, "I keen. I keen for my father who would be joyful and for my mother, who has never known how."

"Just a minute, buster," I said.

And I thought hotly of Gay's face when she was happy, even if the good times often were brushed with anxiety. The last time I won the poetry prize, she thought that she was pregnant. After we graduated, we didn't know what we were going to live on, literally. When we found out, Len was far away at a war it hadn't occurred to him not to attend.

But then I remembered the day Charley was born.

That was a good year. At Stevens and Sons it had been decided that Len was not only good enough but very good indeed, and he had earned a secretary of his own. There was not much left after the month's bills were paid, but the month's bills were paid. They had moved from the hot little flat near Porter Square to the big gracious half-house on Linnaean Street. Len didn't have an ulcer, after all.

Then Charley came.

He came as a posterior presentation and Gay was torn and stitched up again and for the first eight hours they kept her heels higher than her head; she was stuffed like a turkey and everywhere she had a natural aperture there was a tube inserted and where she had none one had been created. Len and I weren't worried, not really, because nobody dies of childbirth anymore or, at least, not at Richardson House.

"Wouldn't you say that?" we both asked the doctor.

"Oh, I don't know," he said. He was a young doctor who still enjoyed the unpredictability of death and life. He said, "I don't think you could find a reputable doctor who'd say there's anything that can't ever happen." He rocked a little on his heels. "But usually it doesn't. Your wife's just fine."

And he let us peek while she was in intensive care. Her curls were brassy with sweat and her lashes were like bruises against her white cheeks.

"Isn't she beautiful," Len said.

Hours later we saw her in her room. She blazed with joy.

Which made me a bit belligerent with Charley. What the hell did he know yet about grief and joy?

At the door I told him, "No, you can't come in.

You've had quite enough. And I've had quite enough."

Charley started singing, which is a thing I could have wished to have been spared at that conservative hotel.

You can easily see she's not my mother —

Charley has a strong voice. He leaned down (he didn't have to lean far down) and kissed my cheek with his smooth young lips.

"Don't be mad," he said.

And then he put his hands on my shoulders and gently rocked me back and forth, and he sang again.

She's just a personal friend of mine!

I stood there chattering with anger and watched him shamble off back toward the Yard, his shoulders hunched into the wind and that terrible pea jacket flopping, and then I went upstairs and lay for a long time watching the shadows of the dry leaves move across the wall.

Charley, I know I'm not your mother. You didn't have to rub it in.

Of course I didn't tell Gay. And it wasn't because I was covering up for Charley; it would have frightened her. She never did understand drinking for fun — she never got the hang of it.

Whereas from the first, Len and I had a natural bent for that pastime.

I don't mean that we drank much in college, but we

had all had a fling at it before. Len and I had each had a couple of boozy evenings in someone else's car with someone else retching on the running board. And Gay had once come across a pint in that brown bathroom, and having taken it away to protect the grandfather she naturally drank it all out of passionate protest and curiosity, which is why she cannot drink brandy to this day.

But none of us drank on campus. Well, Gay didn't and I didn't either, except for that one disastrous occasion. It was too risky. We knew a couple of girls in the dormitory who had some kind of an arrangement with the night watchman — they used to let down a basket and pull up beer, and as far as I know, they were never caught. I always wondered what they did with the bottles.

But we were very much trusted. Well — Gay was very much trusted. After our freshman year we were allowed a corner room on the fire escape and the dean was perfectly right — except for real emergencies, Gay wouldn't let anyone come and go that way. She made it very plain that she was not to be disturbed either at work or rest, and that if it came to expulsion, she was not the one who was going to be expelled. So much for that.

And besides, liquor is expensive, and if Charley thinks we nit-pick, perhaps he doesn't understand how very little cash we had. And what we had or could acquire, we hoarded for vacations. Gay typed and filed for the sociology department, which eventually ended in a small personal crisis. I waited tables, which was euphemistically called being "on trays." This paid peanuts, but you got a substantial reduction on your board. There were no men's dormitories at that time, so the men lived in rooming houses all around town, and lived largely on peanut butter. When Len was low in funds he gave up his current room and moved in, for the nonce, with some friend. This worked well, until everyone caught on — after that, for a week or two before vacations, the whole men's division played Puss-in-the-Corner.

With our ill-gotten gains, we splurged when we went to Boston. In Boston, we always stayed at Bellevue Avenue; Gay's grandmother came to expect me and with all those uncles, Len's presence was more or less unnoticed. I don't think it occurred to us that the S. S. Pierce bill must have gone way up. We assumed that if you were older, you had the wherewithal. Otherwise, what was the point in being older?

We never stayed at my aunt's house. It was too small to be up to whatever you were being up to. I always spent one afternoon there, when my aunt cracked jokes and proffered anxious advice and pressed root beer upon me because she claimed I had always liked root beer. I itched until I got away.

I wonder now if she perhaps hoped we would all come, and maybe made some little plans about it: hamburger buns and the current record hit. The young aren't cruel. They just don't know anything.

I explained how educational it was in Cambridge and she agreed, and it was right about then that she cooked up a lot of educational places where she went herself — Washington, D.C., and Williamsburg, to see the restoration. I hope she really went and if she went, I hope she took somebody with her.

And if she went alone, I hope she took my father's flask.

But we were about our own affairs. Afternoons, we did more or less what Gay wanted to do. We went back again to the glass flowers; they are really amazing and once you have granted that, so what? They are still glass. And we went to Mrs. Jack Gardner's Palace. Len liked the roofed central court and the way you sat in midwinter with the scent of blossoming things about you and the sound of strings playing. Gay liked the Giorgione head of Christ. It is a lovely simple thing: just the top of the cross made of fresh wood and the wounded eyes. But I think what she really liked was the idea of the violets that are always kept in front of it. What I liked was the portrait of Mrs. Jack herself with her matchless arms outstretched, a *jolie laide* (I liked to think) like me. We all liked to think of her scrubbing the church steps on her knees, in Lent. Before that head of Christ even Len was reverent and uneasy. I think the kids might feel that way today if it weren't for the new liturgies. I heard a priest the other day (on TV) who said Christ walked upon the waters and his disciples were afraid. Do you know what Christ said, according to this priest? He said, "Get ahold of yourselves." I don't suppose the priests can help it; they say what they are told to say. But they've sure lost a lot of us.

We went to the Fine Arts, too, though we never committed a luncheon there. There was a small Cézanne of apples on a white cloth with a blue paring knife that made us understand (suddenly) what painting was all about. And a tall *Isabella and the Pot of Basil,* a bad sentimental picture but dear to Gay and me because that year we were very big on Keats. At that age it is hard to resist one whose name is writ in water — it is later when you want something a bit more substantial.

Len liked the sarcophagi.

We all liked the little basement stores along Huntington Avenue where the art students bought their canvas boards and their tubes of ultramarine and their articulated mannequins.

Nights, we pub-crawled in a small way.

We liked to start at the Merry-Go-Round at the Copley Plaza, where we drank very strange things — Pink Ladies or pousse-café, of which it was rumored that one could, legally, be served only one. And then there was the Silver Dollar Bar, which was raunchy and where you ordered beer because you could drink it from the bottle and nobody cared to drink from the glasses. It was outside the Silver Dollar that Gay had to be led around the block because of general dizziness. After that she stuck to a single sherry, which takes a patience with the habits of others that I would never have. But then, even as now, Gay did gaily and gracefully anything Len wanted to do. Unless she thought what he wanted to do was wrong.

Which brings me to sociology.

For some reason you couldn't graduate from our college without two years of physical education and two semesters of sociology. In physical education one wore blue tunics and blue shorts and was urged to leap at balls by an elderly maiden in a blue tunic and blue bloomers. Gay and I were adept at pleading cramps and were allowed to withdraw from volleyball to a sheltered corner of the gymnasium where we played shuffleboard until the assistant, who was just out of Sargent and all efficiency, caught on and began to keep a small notebook in which our periods were recorded. I suppose that is why her contract was renewed.

There was no way out of sociology.

Midyears were on us, and Len and I had absorbed nothing except that there was a family named Jukes and another named Kallikak, which was not really enough to have absorbed. But we weren't worried because Gay worked in the office and had access to the files where the exams were kept.

"You don't seriously mean that?" she asked.

We certainly seriously did.

She said it was immoral and we said it was expedient. She said expediency was the root of evil and we said it was the root of success. She decided we were joking and began to laugh. We weren't joking one bit.

Later Len said, "Do you realize we both could flunk out?"

Gay stood up and tied her scarf under her chin. In those days we were not afraid of looking Russian. She gathered her mittens and her canvas notebooks and her texts.

"All right," she said, "flunk out." And from her tone, she might just as well have said, "Fuck off."

Where was I?

15

Oh.

Gay went into the bathroom and while she was gone, I had just a small bit of the Jack Daniels. When she came out she said, "I like our dresses. Don't you like our dresses?" And then she said, "You know that Len loves Charley. It's just that he doesn't understand."

She turned on the lamps.

That's not it, I thought. It's not that he doesn't understand. He just doesn't remember.

In our Junior year, Len and Gay broke up.

It was that God-awful period in late February when the drama of exams is over, the all-night sessions and the gone-in-the-stomach, over-the-top feeling that comes when they distribute the blue-books and close the doors and the professor chalks the time upon the board. I've asked around and haven't found a B.A. yet who doesn't still have nightmares (and I don't speak figuratively) about not being able to find the room where the exam is to be given or about realizing at the last moment that he has not once attended the course. My own version of this general trauma is that the course that I have not once attended has something to do with history and that since I am a very fast reader, if I could only get hold of the text I might be able to pull it off. With the help of Clio.

Anyway, after exams everyone is surly.

And in late February spring vacation seems light-years away, the weather is mean, coats steam unpleasantly in the vestibule and snow gets into your overshoes; you are sick to death of coffee and of everyone in the smoking room, the movies are all second-run and there is no place else to go.

Except Louie's.

Louie's was the one beer joint where everyone went, always had, probably do now. It was a sprawling, murky place with a long bare bar and time-blackened booths carved with initials and class numerals. At Homecoming and reunions the elderly flocked to Louie's; at other times there was no one there but students.

The factory hands had their own place down by the river where you were supposed to be able to pick up the town girls, though about that, I'm sure I can't say. And the grand place in town was the Seagull Room at the hotel where, we understood, the cloths were linen, the waitresses on their toes, and where on Saturday nights there was a man who sort of played on the piano.

We certainly couldn't afford that kind of thing. So where we went was Louie's.

At Louie's there was a jukebox and the waiters were burly, but for the most part Louie did his own bouncing. The rules were simple: no charging and no disturbances.

Once you were bounced you did not get back in. The place was usually decorous because nobody wanted to take the chance: Louie's was the only place where they didn't ask your age. There was a rumor that Louie had some arrangement with the police. I don't know — maybe it was so. We certainly had an unspoken arrangement with the faculty — we didn't go where they could be seen drinking, and they didn't come to Louie's.

That year Len and two other boys were much envied because they were living in a ramshackle apartment directly over Louie's. I assume it was ramshackle. Gay and I had never been up there, you bet. This was partly because of Gay's determination to keep one step ahead of the dean of women and partly because although there were plenty of girls who went to the boys' rooms, we thought it common; there is a place and time for everything. Gay felt this so strongly that it made her uneasy even to go to Louie's. She felt the proximity of Len's quarters was suggestive. I thought that was nonsense.

Well. So it was February, when Len dropped out of sight.

At first, Gay didn't think much about it. He didn't go to classes, but he had a way of using up his cuts. Gay herself was permitted unlimited cuts and never used any of them, which both Len and I thought was unreasonable.

The second day she was troubled. She thought he might be sick. His roommates said, evasively, that he was fine. Gay asked them to have Len call her, but he didn't call. The boys had no telephone, but if he couldn't come downstairs to the phone booth, didn't that prove that he was sick? She jumped every time the bell rang, but the girl on bells never asked for her.

The third day she was frightened.

That was a long day. It was wet with a nasty something that was more than mist and less than rain and our overheated room was fuggy with drying scarves. Our goosenecked lamps made two hot yellow circles. Gay snapped because I hadn't made my bed. She had called the men's infirmary and they had no record of Len; she was scared and confused. She wouldn't go down to dinner, so we munched some apples I had traded with a girl down the hall for my American Literature notes. I thought we got the better of that bargain. Then we stayed at our desks pretending to be immersed in Wordsworth, which one can be, once in a while. Actually, I quite liked

I thought of Chatterton, the marvelous boy,
The sleepless soul who perished in his pride . . .

Gay preferred *Duty, stern daughter of the voice of God.* That figured.

The message came at nine o'clock and Gay wouldn't take the call.

"Well," I said, "do you mind if I do?"

She didn't care what I did.

As soon as I heard him, I knew something was badly wrong. His voice didn't sound like him and what he said didn't sound like him. Not at all.

He said, "I'm at Louie's. Tell my girl to get on down here."

"At this hour?" I said. "Fat chance."

"Get on down," he said. "Or else I'm coming there."

"Listen," I said, "I don't think she wants to talk to you right now."

"She'll talk to me," Len said, "Or I'll drag her out by her pretty hair."

Which was nonsense, of course. But he was perfectly capable, I decided, of showing up and making some kind of a scene; that would be the last thing in the world Gay needed. And then the dean might forbid him calling privileges, and then there would be all that.

"I'll do what I can," I said.

"I really think maybe we'd better," I told her. She looked at me, her eyes wide. "Gay," I said, "I think he's in some kind of trouble." She kept on looking at me, and then she saw I meant it. So we put on our wet scarves and our damp coats and signed out and went downtown in the black wet night.

I didn't know as much then as I knew just a year or two later; I was always a quick learner. But I knew right away what Len's trouble was. It was simple. He was drunk. He was drunker than anyone I had ever seen at Louie's, which made me wonder if anyone upstairs had had a fifth. His roommates were there but they weren't sitting with him and they had a guilty look, as if they had provided him with something they shouldn't have or had concealed something they shouldn't have. But someone was sitting in the booth with him, and that was a faculty member.

I have never held much with faculty-student socializing and neither has Gay. If nothing dangerous is going to come of it, it's too dull to be borne: the coffee, Coke or punch routine and the doggedly intellectual conversation with its agile avoidance of personalities. All other confrontations are fraught with peril, or they were in our day. The faculty member is the student's natural enemy and if he lets down his guard he is sorry for it later, has a conscience crisis, and feels he has to turn you in. Unless he has prejudiced his own case so badly that he doesn't wish to call administrative attention to what now appears to be a mutual folly; in this case sullen silence ensues. You may have been teacher's pet before the weekend, but try to get an A in the course after Monday. Just try it. This is known as academic integrity. We were aware of it early in the game and gave them all a wide berth. Well, almost all.

The individual at Len's table was a peculiarly sinister type, an assistant professor who had not been at our college long and was not likely to remain. Since his attitudes have become somewhat fashionable, I assume that wherever he went he was up and off to better things. We all knew him as a courter of student affection, as if being best-beloved beat scholarship as the quickest path to tenure. He had a reputation for inviting certain pets to his apartment where, if you were foolhardy enough to accept, rumor said he served you beer, which the trustees would certainly not have liked.

I realize that it's all different now. At one campus I know (I have no reason to suspect they vary) the students give cocktail parties for the faculty, and at another, if the faculty will only entertain the students, they may submit their liquor bills to the bursar. After the way of genius, Mr. Fox was before his time. But I'm not talking about now, I'm talking about then.

Needless to say, Mr. Fox was delighted to see us and offered to buy a beer. And needless to say, neither of us accepted. I know when I'm licked, and Gay's uncompromising face allowed no leeway.

"Thank you," she said. "No."

I think she was still hoping that he would think Len sober. But nobody would have taken Len for sober.

At any rate, this Mr. Fox urged you to drop in at his apartment, which was the usual affair of remodeled rooms in an old house, where he wanted the kids to feel perfectly at home. He also wanted them to notice the copy of the *PMLA* to which he had contributed a few notes concerning *The Pardoner's Tale*. After that he would draw you out, and if you were foolish enough to confide to him your early sorrows, he met you on campus thereafter with a direct look of compassion that was brutal as blackmail. What's more, before the week was out the dean would call you in for a little chat and want to know if there was anything on your mind that you would like to talk about. No, Mr. Fox was not a good man.

How do I know all this? Oh, hearsay. The three of us had not seen that apartment. No.

Nevertheless, Len didn't have to let him know just what we thought.

Len had a strange way of showing drunkenness — still does. His coordination is superb and his enunciation doesn't change at all. What changes is what he enunciates. Later we would have recognized that the dominant mood that night was truculence, but we had never seen him drunk before.

His dark hair spilled across his forehead, but his eyes were steady as steel. He didn't even turn to look at Gay, but he did reach for her hand and while she pretended that it wasn't happening, he kneaded it. I suppose he was saying, "I am more of a man than you. I have a woman. This is she." That type of thing is not flattering to a lady unless she is very basic. Gay is not that basic.

You will say this is all hindsight. It certainly is.

Drinking is not an art that one ever masters, no matter how assiduous one's efforts, but there are certain basic errors you can avoid. Like rage. No, Gay had never seen Len drunk before, but if you know one you know them all. The grandfather was a plaintive man and not an angry one, but Gay was not interested in how the symptoms varied. She removed her hand from Len's and suggested that he walk us back to the dorm.

"Certainly not," Len said.

Mr. Fox asked if we would reconsider and have a beer. He was avid with interest, the way people are who have little life of their own. He said, meaning I'm sure to be engaging, "I won't tell."

And then he made a large mistake. Eyeing Len and Gay in a prurient fashion he said slyly, "A little town like this is hard on you young people. Remember, my latchkey's always out."

"Thank you," Len said. "We're not that hard up."

That's where the quarrel really started, though neither of them took the guards off the foils at that point. In fact, when the shouting began it was over something quite different, which made a kind of sense since they were both students of English literature and as such (a useful phrase that I abominate) were familiar with the protocol of duels. One never involves the lady's name and when the gauntlet's hurled the cause is always arbitrary.

The conversation moved to music. Mr. Fox admired Wagner. Len sneered. Wagner, Len said, was for the insecure.

Mr. Fox flushed. He wanted to know if Len cared for music.

Len cared very much indeed.

In that case, Mr. Fox would like to know whom Len admired.

Len said there was only one musician.

Mr. Fox presumed that Len was talking about Mozart.

Len was talking about Mozart, but he was not going to admit it. He said he spoke of Haydn.

Mr. Fox said that Haydn tinkled. He said that music should be a deep cry from the heart of man. He really said that. Then he asked what Len was going to do about *Also Sprach Zarathustra.*

Len said that he himself wasn't going to do anything about it, but he had a suggestion about what Mr. Fox could do with it.

Gay looked at her watch.

Mr. Fox wanted to know where on the scale Len would place Purcell.

Len said *Dido and Aeneas* was the greatest opera of all time.

Mr. Fox was tickled. He said that Purcell reflected teacups and fans. He suggested kindly that Len would understand *Zarathustra* better if he familiarized himself with Nietzsche.

The waiter brought them both another beer. Len looked deep into its depth and then, explaining that he didn't like Mr. Fox's opinions nor his attitudes nor his personal habits, he hurled the beer into Mr. Fox's face, and while the poor man groped for his glasses I moved (being quick to spot this kind of thing) and so was standing safely aside when Len tipped the whole table over and punched one of the man's unguarded eyes.

Everyone in that dim room was electrified; no one more than the proprietor. But though in those days Louie was not an elderly man and kept himself in good shape, he was not as quick as we. Gay and I were out on the pavement in a trice and watching while Len's guilt-ridden roommates bumped him up the stairs.

Len wasn't busted. These kids today are poets; their speech is irresistible. What can be more accurate than busted? Or uptight, or letting it all hang out? On the other hand, hangup is not as good as hangover, though either is better than bummer.

Gay said she wasn't worried about it. She said a fairly young faculty member might be able to afford being seen in a bar once; he cannot afford to have his eye blacked in a bar, not even once. And she was right. Mr. Fox went around for a week with dark glasses and said he had conjunctivitis, and of course none of the kids would rat on Len, not wishing to be ratted on in similar circumstances.

But he was busted as far as Gay was concerned.

She wouldn't speak to him, nor would she receive his

emissaries. Both roommates came to plead his cause but had to plead to me, which was rather fun. I met them in the student store and downtown and on the back porch of the dormitory, and the taller of the two went so far as to borrow a car and drive me out of town, where he fumbled a pass. I didn't bother to tell Gay about these efforts in any detail, any more than I would bother to tell Len's false friends why she was adamant. Len didn't need to get the message. He knew. Gay had had it up to here with drunken men.

Eventually Len was able to persuade her that he was not a natural alcoholic (he isn't, either) but a natural experimenter. He said she ought to understand his curiosity, admiring intellectual curiosity as she did. He also said everyone had a right to a second chance.

She said, but not a third.

I suppose I sound flippant, but it was all a very long time ago. He never got drunk again, as far as I know, at least not until after they were married.

16

MANY A MARRIAGE has endured because of congenial drinking habits.

Most of us like our drinks and if the truth were known get a bit restless just before the cocktail hours. But Gay says drinking is a waste of time and a withdrawal from reality, which seems to me both true and perfectly dandy.

Anyway, Gay has her own method of withdrawing. She's never without a book and I have seen her iron with Simone de Beauvoir on the ironing board, wash dishes with "Samson Agonistes" propped between the faucets, and entertain guests with her eyes sliding toward the latest *Saturday Review*. Yesterday — remember we hadn't seen each other for two years — she was carrying a large straw bag filled with fine things from the Boston Public Library and while she bathed, I knew that one of them was perched precariously beside her.

That large straw bag accompanied us last night, which somewhat gave me pause, though it held nothing by then but her evening bag and the current *Harper's*. Here she was, all slippered and satined and wearing the bright red lipstick that seems about to be fashionable again — and hauling a large straw carryall that looked as if she had been to market. Gay thinks me unconventional in many ways, but I would never carry a thing like that for an evening on the town. On the other hand, in Boston after dark you can always lay your hand on a drink, but even in Boston it is not always possible to lay your hand on a *Harper's*.

Maybe it was the one drink she had from my flask. One good thing about drinking very little is that when you do drink, it takes very little. Sam and I were speaking about this just the other day. We buy our liquor by the case so that we won't get nervous about running out, and we buy the big half-gallon bottles so we won't have to go back and forth to the pantry. The other night after a normal cocktail session, a rather good dinner and a pleasant sleep, I pointed out that we had done away with a half of a half gallon. Since there had been no blows and no sobbing in the night I don't suppose it was important, but if you figure it up, I suppose we spend on liquor in a month what a semester's tuition used to be. There is some moral issue involved here which I should like to think out, if I have the time.

Behold us in our finery. Our throats are bare. I wear my rubies, Gay the diamond pendant I have never seen her without since Len gave it to her on their fifteenth anniversary. We are both sleeved; at our age it is better. Neither of us needs a girdle. Neither of us has a fur. She did not expect to be out this evening, and I am not about to take my sable. I have left it behind too often and had to go back. Once, in the morning, Sam found it on a bush.

While we were still deciding who should take the key, the phone rang again.

I felt danger, hot at my heels. "Don't answer it," I said.

"I have to," she said reasonably. "It might be John."

But it was only Wes, wondering where Len was. Someone knocked at the door and Gay said, "He's here."

The dangers of martinis before lunch are obvious. But Len, fresh-shaven and clear-eyed and smelling a little too strongly of Canoe, was ready for anything.

"Practice makes perfect," Gay said.

She meant that martinis before lunch are an occupational hazard; it is a rare day when Len doesn't take some writer to lunch. Writers expect this. Also, each writer thinks he is the only one to be so fêted. Also, writers drink.

"You notice he ate lightly." And come to think of it, he had. There is a limit to how much one can consume and still look lean and youthful. However, that appearance of unlimited endurance was illusory. There are no heroes.

"We'll have one here," Len said.

It was Gay's opinion that if there were time for a drink here, it would be best not to have one, since the time would be better spent in walking to the party — the fresh air would stand us in good stead. And it was rather silly, wasn't it, to pay for a round here?

Len said, "But Marta's meeting us in the lounge."
There was a swift silence.

Then Gay said only, "Oh?"

I knew who Marta was, of course. I had not thought
to meet her.

When her name began to be scattered through Gay's
letters, she was a very new junior editor straight out of
Smith. In a distressingly short time she was Len's assistant. When Gay decided that she disliked Marta, she
searched her soul. Could it be she was jealous? And if
jealous, was it because she coveted the Smith degree, or
the career that she herself had never had? It certainly had
nothing to do with Len.

When she stopped mentioning Marta, I assumed she
had settled these questions to her own satisfaction.

By day, the second floor cocktail lounge at the Ritz
is uninhabited except for a few ladies with hats who have
just barely made it back from Bonwit's. The few lamps
glow but wanly. Hotels, like people, look best at night.
Last night every table bloomed with light, the deep blue
carpet garlanded with roses looked rich and reliable;
against it the scarlet leather of the chairs and banquettes
burned. There are great square pillars in that room, for
some reason, and behind one of them someone was playing the piano. Everywhere martinis glinted like dia-
monds. In such rooms, at such hours, I always feel a
stirring of excitement. No matter what experience has
taught me, I believe at such times in comradeship, in
safety, in unspeakable delights. All things are possible.

At a corner table there was waiting for us a slim,

honey-haired young woman dressed in sea-green — one of the coolest young women I am likely to meet, things being as they are. She sat beneath a Copley-ish portrait of a maiden in a mob cap who is holding a handful of paintbrushes and wearing an impractical filmy fichu. I've always liked it because the maiden looks so delighted with herself. I'm sure the other maiden was pleased with herself, too. She was serene, cerebral, serious: My God, I thought. She looks a little bit like Gay.

My friend greeted her with a smile that I know from way back — radiant, brilliant, totally false. The girl returned the look in a way that was totally honest and that scared me to death. Because I saw that Gay was in bigger trouble than she knew. This girl is much too tolerant of Len's wife and if I read her right, much too sure of Len.

She had an air of untroubled possession that made me want to smack her. One saw that she was perfectly willing to render unto Caesar's wife that which was Caesar's wife's — her home, her children, her place in the connubial bed. What she implied was that these things were not important. What she implied was that if she hadn't yet taken them it was because she didn't want them yet. This is the result of letting women into business.

Like Gay and not like her. She has a creamy throat that rises like a stalk from that understated dress, her little head is swathed in hair, not cropped. But the real difference is that Gay's calm is the calm of self-control, Marta's of self-possession. And every time she moved (she moved very slightly, and usually just to allow Len to light her cigarette) she might just as well have shouted, *why don't you go home?* Gay was back with her Dubonnet. Marta didn't order anything; Len ordered for her. The lady likes vermouth on the rocks.

I have never minded Gay's Dubonnet. I have never liked people who drink vermouth on the rocks. It indicates that they are superior people who, unlike the rest of us, have no need for stimulants, and they can consume innumerable vermouths and remain superior while the rest of us go happily to pieces. She is an attractive young woman, though. Oh, yes she is.

Even Wes, that clown, noticed this and turned attentive; Wes has never been able to resist attractive women. I bit my lip — a useful phrase, though I have never actually seen anyone bite his lip. But it was not because of Wes. One notices much trivia when one does not notice that one is noticing; and right now I was putting a few things together. Len could have shaved in Wes's room but he hadn't; if he had, Wes wouldn't have called to ask where he was because he would have known. He might have gone to the barbershop but they don't hand out clean shirts at the barbershop. So wherever he went it was someplace where he kept a razor and clean shirts. And she certainly hadn't left the office in a sea-green gown. How cozy.

"And where do you live, Marta?" I asked.

She gave me a brief smile. "I have a little place on Joy Street."

"How nice for you," I wanted to say. And, "How appropriate." I also wanted to ask her, "Didn't you have a dear Papa of your very own?" But there are things you don't say until later in the evening and even then, only if you are pretty sure no one is going to remember.

Besides, I don't claim prescience. I could be wrong. Although I don't know how.

So I addressed myself to my drink. Martinis on the rocks look seemly and almost everyone orders them to show that they're not all that serious about the matter at hand, but if what you want is that first sharp promising sip you have to be about it because the ice melts, and while they will do the trick if you stay with them, they don't taste very good. The thing to do is to drink them rather quickly and then sip patiently at the icewater while you are waiting for your friend. Len seemed to think so, too.

While I sipped patiently I noticed that the paint on the white panel beside me was slightly chipped and that the cord to our standing lamp was frayed in a fashion that made me think gratefully of those competent guards that patrol the Ritz from nine to six, which are just the hours that you get your careless parties and your fiends. Perhaps it is because I have been living in the West where things are brash and new, but I am always surprised to find the great hotels in the East just a little shabby. No matter how resplendent the name, the paint is always chipped. The last time I was in New York, at the Plaza, the bedspreads were darned.

I don't know why it is, but two out of three women are unable to leave one place for another place without the ladies' room. Perhaps it is for the comfort of being in advance of need. Perhaps it is for the satisfaction of knowing how you look. At any rate, about now Marta covered her glass with her slim, creamy hand (a gesture I find infuriating) and speaking quietly to Len, she said it was time we were on our way. Gay and I glanced at one another and arose.

Sam always says — I miss Sam; he is good company — that women's most significant conversations take place in bathrooms. He has noticed this. He says that at every party two or three always cluster there for much longer than can possibly be necessary, and he is almost right. But three can only cluster, and only two can talk. Three women chat about diets and schools. Only two can discuss other women, which is what I think Sam thinks they do. Well, men have their locker rooms. The third woman left at a table does know that she is likely to be talked about, but if she is one of those who pretends that she never has to go, she has to take her chance. Whatever Marta may have thought, when Gay and I withdrew, her name did not come up.

That ladies' room is of staggering simplicity, colorless as a bus station although cleaner, and it doesn't seem to have been refurbished in any way since 1928, when the hotel was built. Even then it seemed better to discourage the ladies from combing their hair over the washbasins, though you wouldn't think that with all those bobs the drains would suffer much, so a section is provided where you sit before mirrors and it is there that the maid, in her black dress and white apron, presides. I am always nervous for fear I haven't a quarter to give her in case she does some little thing for me before I can prevent it, like handing me a paper towel that I could perfectly well reach. Tonight, however, she was doing a crossword puzzle and didn't even look up and we sailed by her without flinching.

I tucked a loose lock of hair behind my ear and then I pulled it out again. I keep forgetting that right now those loose locks are supposed to be attractive. Gay jerked her comb through her short curls and then she sighed and said, "This is the anniversary of my grandmother's death."

When Gay and I first met we talked a lot about death, as the young will, and were much moved by lines about sorrow and early loss—ah, many a time we wept for Adonais. But we don't talk about it much anymore—I mean, what's to say? And it was certainly not a topic I would have chosen for the agenda that last night. Besides, I was away when the grandmother died, and though we had become friends, I couldn't be expected to remember the very day and didn't pretend to.

I simply said flatly, "Is that so."

"It was a perfect marriage," she had the nerve to say. "They were devoted. After he died she used to have these dreams that he was coming after her."

It didn't sound like devotion to me, not the way I like to think of it. "I knew them both. Remember?" But at the same time I was remembering that moment of revelation in the upstairs hall when I had seen that, indeed, they needed one another.

I saw that Gay was a little angry with me. It is perfectly possible to be a little angry with a friend. "I know what you mean by that," she said. "But it's a very superficial thing to say. They stayed together and they may have had their spats. But nothing disturbed that marriage, not ever. Not from the outside."

So perhaps we weren't talking about death at all.

But then she said, "They're buried side by side. It rained the day of both funerals."

"Look," I told her, "I sort of planned to have a few laughs tonight."

I feel if you lay low and say nothing you stand a better chance of not attracting the attention of the Fates. The fact that I know this is not true has nothing to do with the fact that I believe it.

Our eyes met coldly. "Laughter doesn't solve everything," she said.

"It doesn't hurt," I said. "What you need is a proper drink."

So we painted our lips again because whatever impression we made on the men, we would make right now. By dinnertime they wouldn't notice if every scrap were gone, but might remember us as we looked now. We gathered up our bags and combs and lipsticks.

I went forth eagerly. Behind me Gay stalked grimly, swinging the big straw bag. Before we emerged from behind the big brown screen, she paused and spoke argumentatively.

"Len loves his sons," she said. "He loves them very much."

17

LORD. I know that.

Sometimes I think I saw the pattern before Gay did, because she was very busy at the time. Or maybe—and in this case I don't come off too well—I just want to be the one who saw it first because I saw him first. In spite of the immaculate manners, Len has a lot of pent-up violence, and it is always love that releases it. Love and fear.

I think perhaps a lot of men are like that, though I know that like the rest of us, they come in many shapes and sizes. But since there are no saber-tooths to fight, some men do fight for the endangered one in curious ways, and Len is one of them. If Mr. Fox had not with an insinuation impugned Gay's honor — and doesn't that sound quaint — he would not have sustained that black eye. If Charley had not endangered himself, Gay would not have asked me not to mention him.

John has always been a tractable child — or used to be; I've given up predicting. He arrived when the doctor said he would and gave his mother no sass. But during Gay's second pregnancy Len and I were worried. Gay said we were ridiculous, that she had no intention of making a habit of having a hard time. She said that this time it was Len who was going to get the short end of the deal, and she was right.

I understand that nowadays they have you up and and on your feet before the anesthetic has well cleared from your head if you are one who has not opted for natural childbirth, and that it is a lazy girl indeed who isn't wheeled out of the hospital on the third day. Back then it took that long before they let you dangle, which meant sitting on the side of your bed for a few minutes, dizzy and sick, with your feet hanging pale and slight. You didn't leave till the tenth day, but you left on your feet.

It did make problems for the young wife who had no mother, sister or aunt. I had a puny job that year but one I needed very much, and I could not play aunt or sister. But the head of the firm (he was really not a bad old man) said Len could have leave and furthermore, didn't have to consider it his vacation. Len had no reason to consider it his vacation. The head of the firm kept up on things and knew that at the time you couldn't get help for love or money. Gay and Len still had a lot more love than money.

Len did all right. Many a man has done worse. The house went to pot and he was harried and unshaven, but nothing really went wrong for several days. I looked in every day and gave him hints which he took fairly well.

Like suggesting that even after chicken is cooked it's better kept in the refrigerator, and that when a two-year-old regresses to painting with his feces it is because he is insecure and not because he loathes his father. Len said that he himself would never have done such a thing unless he loathed his father, and I pointed out that he had never had a father, not to mention, and couldn't possibly say. Len pointed out in return that I had never had a child and for a moment or two things were pretty tense between us, but then Charley fell down in the bathtub.

The next day I was held up in town with a disputed wisdom tooth and got to the house late. I had had sense enough to lie to Gay and tell her I was a witness and that everything was fine. But when I had climbed from the clanking streetcar, and walked the shady length of Linnaean Street, I knew everything was not fine because even from outside I could hear Charley crying.

There is nothing that hurts like a child who cries and cannot be comforted, because he cannot explain why he cries and you cannot explain why he should be comforted. They are very heavy and hot and their hair gets wet.

Len was trying to rock him in the battered Hitchcock rocker that had been Gay's grandmother's, but the child arched and stiffened against him and it was perfectly easy to see why. Len's face was white with anger, and a successful rocker has to be relaxed. Children can tell.

I said, "What happened?"

Len said, "I struck him."

I said, "You mean you spanked him."

Len said, "No. I struck him."

And Charley put a small fat hand over his ear and said, "Here."

That got to me. You don't hit a child anywhere except on the buttocks where it smarts but can't hurt anything and because every child knows that is what a bottom is for. No child understands being hit about the head.

"But *why?*"

They had gone shopping in Porter Square. Len had bought milk and bread and cigarettes and a small plastic truck for Charley and then they walked to the big Sears Roebuck store where Len was looking for a washer for a leaking faucet and when he went to pay for it he shifted the paper parcel from one arm to the other and he let go Charley's hand for a moment and then Charley wasn't there. He wasn't in the next aisle either or anywhere on that floor and Len thought he might be riding on the escalator but he wasn't, and when Len reached the street with his heart banging and the brass taste of terror in his mouth he looked to right and left and Charley wasn't there, either.

Porter Square is not a good place to lose a child. The traffic is fast and heavy and the cars and trucks and streetcars shoulder each other angrily. There is an attractive bridge over the railroad tracks from which a small boy could fall or under which he could be trapped with a train coming. And there are those deluded dangerous women who want children. And then there are the others . . .

Len had dashed in and out of stores and had confronted strangers and had at last found a policeman (who had not heard of any accident) and then in desperation started up his own street looking in every entry and alley and finally got to his own house where Charley was waiting for him on the steps, having done the only thing an intelligent child who is lost can do. Crossing the avenue and the railroad bridge and all the side streets and watching anxiously for landmarks, he had gone home. Frightened at being separated, halfway there he had abandoned the small plastic truck.

So I could understand why Len had struck him. I'm sure Charley understood it, too, long ago, if he remembers it at all. But at the moment Charley didn't understand and I'm not sure that Len did either and they were having a hard time with quite a different sort of separation.

Charley straightened in his father's arms. His lashes were stuck together and his ear was pink. He wailed, "I don't like it!"

I wanted to take the baby (because he wasn't much more than a baby) into my arms and comfort him with the unfair advantage of my femaleness: my warmth and scent and softness. But that would have been mean, so instead I stood there feeling like a false friend and a false godmother.

Charley said it again. "I don't like it!"

And, thank God, Len understood. He didn't mean he didn't like Len and he didn't even mean that he didn't like being lost. He meant he didn't like things coming so fast and so new and his mother gone.

Len's arms tightened around him. He said, "I don't like it either, chum."

Charley's head dropped on Len's shoulder, and since there was nothing I could do except be in the way I turned and left them rocking and hanging onto one another in their rage and grief.

Gay had a perfect girl-child with blue lids and smoky lashes. They tried to change all her blood, but in a few days she died. She was to have been named for me.

Gay never speaks of her.

18

THE ONE TIME I came close to finishing a book I had (because of Len) an audience with a man who was probably going to become a senior editor. Naturally, he did not take me to the Ritz. He did give me a drink at the apartment where he lived with Mother. Mother wasn't there, but I don't think she had left because of me.

This editor was much attached to Dickens, which did not seem to damage his abilities. The whole apartment — the rooms were large, low-ceilinged and dim with that particular grey light that filters through oily windows on the Hill — was filled with evidence of his taste: complete sets in lovesome limp red leather, a few first editions, small winning figurines of much-loved characters and reproductions of the illustrations by Phiz. I particularly liked Mr. Pickwick sliding on the ice and Silas Wegg reading *The Decline and Fall off the Roman Empire*. But it did make you wonder if he had any personal life.

He liked my book, if that is what it was, but pointed

out that the last third was weak, in fact, that the last third was missing. I felt that this was captious criticism, since in those days I thought that if you got a whole bunch of characters that far along they were bound to finish up by themselves, just as they would in real life. What I didn't understand was that in real life people seldom die or fail or triumph at the right time, and that they almost never coordinate their ends with those of others. So that if you just let them alone and hope for the best, the result is going to be as unsatisfying as it is when you just look around you.

He very kindly let me use Mother's bathroom. She favored English soaps.

That nice man is no longer with the firm, though I forget just why. I have a feeling that eventually he threw his cap over the mill and was off to the remote Bermudas. Upon the few occasions when I got to attend publication parties I was glad that he wasn't present because only he and Len knew that I had almost failed because I had almost tried. We human beings are not very nice, are we.

But I do love those parties. The hors d'oeuvres, both hot and cold, resemble those at any cocktail party and so do the drinks and so, alas, does much of the conversation. But the people — ah, they are of a race apart. They make books. And whether their primary interest is in printing costs or advertising schedules or subsidiary rights or even in literature, they all believe that making books is a reasonable thing to do. What's more, a few of them seem to believe in authors, though to be fair, most authors' belief in themselves is so arrogant (however disguised by a winning childishness) that they don't really need these parties, which are after all only the outward and visible sign of an inner grace. But they enjoy them.

Last night's party was a small one, as they go. We were so to speak *en famille*. There were no reporters present, no famous guests and only one reviewer. This was partially because it is hard to get excited over Larry Lawrence's fourteenth novel. Lawrence himself, with a very pale, very tall drink in which all the ice had melted, looked bored to death once he had counted the house.

And speaking of houses. It is not unusual for publishers to call themselves a House, but Stevens and Sons really is one. It is a thin building on Commonwealth that shares its sidewalls with its neighbors and that so slants with age that I always wonder whether the narrow stairs or the creaking elevator will collapse first. What used to be bedchambers are now offices and what was the withdrawing room is where we gather at these times. It is a large room, not without its charm, with a faded Chinese oriental rug and walls that are lined with bookshelves in which repose the firm's past triumphs. I am happy to say there are a lot of them. The furniture is old and tasteful and the whole gracious effect only slightly marred by the receptionist's cubbyhole and her telephone board with all its snaking wires.

Though I have never seen that *sanctum sanctorum*, I happen to know that what was once the dining room is now a conference room. I assume there is no longer any kitchen as such, though there must be some space from which the caterers function. Upstairs, the offices go in an ascending order of importance — copy editors and art department on the second floor, editors on the third, and administrative offices on the fourth. I am sorry to say that there is a certain amount of ill-feeling between floors.

I greeted the guest of honor, with whom I had had a brushing acquaintance once before and achieved a martini (I don't mean to complain, but I think the martinis were Heublein's) and then I looked around bemused and bedazzled and, hesitant in a corner and clutching one of those fake-leather binders in which we used to store our theses was a youngish man with great innocent eyes behind heavy glasses, who was just as dazzled as I.

"Who's that?" I asked.

"Oh God, I forgot," Len said. "He's one of mine."

For one who doesn't care for parties, Gay is very good at this sort of thing. She zeroed in on the one who was Len's, talked to him easily and brightly, and then listened with her eyes engaged. She is very good indeed. Later I asked her how come, and she shrugged and said it was all part of the game. Right then it let Len go about his duties. And he had duties, but this little person should not be neglected, because you never know. He didn't look like a best seller, but then they frequently don't. And writers who will put up with ungenerous contracts and insufficient advertising (which is always the fault of the fourth floor) are off like gazelles if they get their feelings hurt.

So Gay charmed Walter Bakerman (such was his name and you may recognize it, later) and Len said, "I'll get you a drink. Martini?"

"Not a martini," Walter said, with some haste.

He had given them up, he said, since a party at which he had abandoned his glasses and his Athenaeum card. But he would have a little wine. Gay would have a little, too. And by the time the waiter reached us Walter couldn't have cared less where Len had gone because he was so enchanted with us ladies. If I do say so.

I liked Walter Bakerman. He was the happiest man I'd seen in weeks. This very day — this very afternoon — Stevens and Sons had accepted his manuscript and in a twinkling, all was changed. His papers had become a manuscript and he himself, an author.

"Of course," he said apologetically, "it's only prose."

Which startled me until I gathered that he distinguished (very properly) between nonfiction and works of the imagination. Nevertheless, it was to be dignified by page proofs, dust jacket and, I hope, notice in the press.

"Jane Avril," he explained.

We were delighted, having at one time been very big on the *belle époque*. Gay quoted a poet of whom we were once passionately fond:

Jane Avril bends her head
Too gaily for a dancer dead . . .

and we were off, with the names flying like ping-pong balls: Rothenstein, the Goncourts, Utrillo, Le Moulin Rouge, Le Chat Noir, Robert de Montesquiou. This is a good name, and I was amused but not surprised that when the waiter came around again they both, absently, exchanged their empty glasses for full ones.

I like to see men at their work. Hosting small parties is of course a very minor part of Len's work, but he does it well, mostly because of that instinctive and captivating courtesy that makes every soul present feel that he is the very one with whom Len wishes to hold speech, even if they have held speech together only an hour before. I have never seen him in the actual act of editing, but I think I know why he is a good editor. He too reveres the Word. He reads with passion and if what he reads is well-written, he can laugh and cry. He also knows what makes others laugh and cry, which is not always the same thing. And he has an unerring sense of pace and form, and, if need be, can show the author where to place the flying buttress without which the most splendid cathedral tumbles. If I had pursued my first ambitions, I should like to have worked with him.

Meanwhile Wes had been paying glum court to the large lady who reviews light fiction for a Boston paper and also has a cooking column. On second thought, I suppose the two are reconcilable. I drifted to his defense, but it was not easy to extricate him. But I did at last and when I did we found that Gay and Walter had shifted corners but not topics.

"And is that *it?*" Gay asked, reverently touching the binder that he clutched beneath his arm.

That was it.

"Goodness," she said. "Are you sure you shouldn't put it somewhere safe?"

"Nowhere is safe enough," Walter said. "This is the only copy."

Fortunately neither Len nor Marta heard. Editors are

enraged with authors who have only this one copy. *Why?* editors want to know. Well, I could tell them. Carbon paper is too hard to deal with. It takes too long and doesn't go into the typewriter right, so that often you have a blank page with mirror-writing on the back. This is no help to anyone. Besides, it is bad joss. Carbon copies assume that you have not just a bunch of papers but a serious effort: I am not the only one who is superstitious.

Still, things are always happening to only copies. They are lost in the mails and left in taxicabs and I have read of at least one that was destroyed by a typhoon, though I don't suppose that would happen often. Haydn's wife used his scores for curling papers, and Carlyle's *History of the French Revolution* was thrown in the fireplace by a thoughtless if not vengeful maid. It is no wonder that editors fret.

Walter's eyes behind the heavy glasses were jubilant; God knows what fine dreams he was dreaming. What a nice small person; I would just as soon see him again someday, if I were going to be around.

These parties don't last long, for good and sufficient reasons. The caterers are paid by the drink and the waiters by the hour and the senior people at the firm all have to get back to Lincoln and Newton. But brief parties are not necessarily safe ones. We once for some reason attended a class reunion. It was not a happy experience. Everyone else had aged too rapidly and no one seemed to be married to the people they used to be married to; when, with low cries of pleasure, we would enquire for Marian or George, our friends looked hurt and reproachful and introduced us to Lily or to Edward. But what I remember most about that reunion was that just one hour had been scheduled for cocktails.

One hour is not enough for cocktails. It may be enough for that handful of nonserious drinkers who hold a glass just for the looks of things, but they are not many. Most of us had taken the precaution of having a few in our rooms, but the foolish virgins with no oil in their lamps had to down drinks so rapidly that by the time we left for dinner a disproportionate number of the class was drunk, and two never achieved the table at all. Gay said it was bestial.

Nothing like that occurred last night. After all, that was a place of business. But by the time the first drifters drifted, I was feeling the gathering excitement and the sense of well-being that is the reward of gin carefully and knowledgeably applied. Larry Lawrence and his editor had left as soon as was decent. Len wanted to go, but I intercepted the stern look Marta gave him. That look said that it was not seemly for either of them to leave until the bitter end, and until the bitter end, we stayed.

At last the room was emptied of all others, and was no more attractive than any room is when the guests have departed, leaving everything slightly out of place, half-munched tidbits of soft crackers and soured cream and the air stale with the smell of imperfectly extinguished cigarettes.

"Let's get out of here," Len said.

Our new friend looked crestfallen. Was it all over, the birthday of his life? Was it to frazzle out, leaving him alone in his room on the seventh floor of the Avery Hotel?

No. Len is very kind. "I tell you what," he said. "You come to dinner with us."

Walter would very much like to. Very much indeed.

That left an awkward gap. Gay said kindly, "You come too, Marta."

"Of course she's coming. It's all arranged," Len said. "Just let me call John first."

Marta was demonstrating how much she was at ease in Zion. She directed the waiters, pointing out a glass that had been abandoned beneath a chair and an ashtray over-looked upon the mantel. Then because Walter was Len's he became by extension, so to speak, one of hers.

She said, "You aren't going to take that with you?"

Walter transferred the binder from under his left arm to under his right. Indeed he was.

"It would be safer if you left it here. I'll put it in my office."

For a gentle man, Walter is very stubborn. "No," he said, and added thoughtfully, "The place might burn."

Well, I knew what he meant. It's my opinion that half Boston could burn at any moment, and if Walter's a fearer of fire, I'm another. I avoid Len's office because after the first floor the stairs are narrow, old and oil-soaked and the elevator is a small open cage that lurches uncertainly between floors. Last time I was up there a siren sounded below and Len rushed to the window with interest to see what was going on, while I froze and trembled. It was only a police car but if it had been a fire engine and Stevens and Sons had been on fire, I never would have made it. There must be fire escapes up there but I have never been able to locate them. I wouldn't be surprised if they were just those little iron balconies that are so popular around that part of town, by which you are supposed to get from flaming room to room or on which you are to wait for the ladder. I don't think much of either notion.

And all along Commonwealth there are hundreds of old houses just like this one, all running together the better to get crackling. Most of them are rooming houses now, or doctors rent them. I suppose the doctors must have some kind of watchmen because of all that valuable equipment but God knows what goes on in the rooming houses, or right here for that matter once we were gone and the waiters started drinking up what was left of the liquor.

"Well," Marta said, "we could stop by your hotel."

He shook his head. "That might burn, too."

Of course she didn't know that it's his only copy.

Watching Marta checking as carefully as if it were her own living room and Gay standing awkward as a departing guest, I had a moment of clairvoyance. These women didn't know the same man. I don't really think Marta wants the same man Gay goes to bed with and I don't think Gay knows the man Marta works with. And suddenly Len was the one I felt sorry for, because maybe he doesn't know which man he is.

It is not easy for Len to refuse affection; I do know that. Not that he needs it, but because affection is as great a thing as anyone can offer, and to refuse it is to belittle the offerer. This is a nice way for men to be, but hard on wives. With my new momentary clarity I watched him clatter down the stairs and saw that something had gone awry. Probably something very slight.

Gay didn't notice. But she did see him pour a last strong drink and down it, and her lips were compressed.

When Gay does not approve of what is going on, she is somewhat less charming than when she does approve. She becomes brittle and sparse, and I know what I mean by this if no one else does. She used to look that way when I cut a class.

She said, "I should have talked to John, too."

Len said, "John is fine, and he knows where we're going to be." And then before our eyes Len changed and became the person I once knew, and neither woman liked it. "Because from here," he said, "we are not going straight to dinner."

That was all right with me. Once you go to dinner the night is over, and I didn't want the night to end. It was all right with Wes too and with Walter. I think I know what Walter felt. Once he was back in that room on the airshaft, the best was over. Whether you succeed or not doesn't make as much difference as you thought it would. There is a moment of glory and after that you are the same person with the same callus on your heel and the same ominous twinge in that back molar.

Gay said we would miss our reservation.

Len had postponed our reservation.

Marta said there was a conference scheduled for the morning.

Len said he would be there.

Both women looked at one another with something

very much like sympathy. And while Marta checked again for unnecessary lights and smoldering cigarettes, Gay helped her.

Then we were on the street and looking for cabs.

It is nice to walk, but Copley Square is a little far from Commonwealth if you have a deadline, and both the ladies had a deadline in their eyes. And six is a nicer number than five because it is pleasant to have the couples come out even.

We were in luck. Not only did two cabs come along, but both drivers seemed to think us harmless. On the whole, Boston cabbies are paranoid, which is not surprising if you read the papers.

Being abstemious is only advantageous up to a certain point — after that it is detrimental. When a man like Len gets going it takes a good deal of experience to keep up with him, and three of us were not qualified. Or that's what I thought.

19

THE Merry-Go-Round, I feel, was a mistake.

I think that like Walter, I should have stuck to prose, and I think the prose I should have written might have been called *Bars I Have Known*. Perhaps it would have lent me only a dubious distinction, but I think it could have had what Stevens and Sons call universal appeal.

As it so chanced, I met Sam in a bar.

We were both leaving Logan airport. Planes scare the hell out of me. There is no reason why things that heavy should stay up and sure enough, once in a while they don't. And mind you, this was before skyjacking.

I was on my way to Wyoming to visit a fairly good friend who had a little hideaway out there in which she hid away once or twice a year. She had been nice to me for a while right after Barry died and before I stopped being fun. I guess she thought that enough time had passed so that I could give and get a laugh again.

Massachusetts Bay was very blue and sparkly that day, just as I understand it was the day the jet took off, sucked all those starlings into the engines and came right down again in the harbor. Quite a few were saved. Another thing I hate is the way you have to pick up your ticket an hour before your flight, so that you have plenty of time to think about these things. The bar at Logan leaves a lot to be desired, but at least you can get your mind off how foolhardy you are to do what you are going to do.

It was Fall — though come to think of it, that only applies properly to the First Fall. Oh, well. It was autumn, and I was wearing a handsome tweed suit and had more alligator going in the way of pumps and purse than I have now that we know there are not all that many alligators left.

Among the nuggets of advice my aunt gave me, there were one or two that concerned drinking places. I was never to rest my elbows on the bar because it would soil my sleeves, and I was never, never to speak to strangers. It didn't occur to me then to wonder how she had come to these conclusions, but then I never did know, not for sure, what she did with her vacations. I am careful about my elbows, but I do speak to strangers. It is more fun that way.

Sam was a stranger and about the shyest man I have ever seen. I'm sure a lot of women would have thought him handsome but what appealed to me was the way he looked baffled and lost. As it turned out, we were not only waiting for the same flight but were headed for the same destination. How about that? How many people, on any given day, do you think are headed for

Jackson Hole, Wyoming? When the flight was called we lost track of one another but once on the plane, damned if we didn't turn out seatmates.

My aunt used to say some things are written in the stars.

Whatever Sam was lost and baffled about, it wasn't flying. I hate the long period while you taxi out and wait in line for your turn to go up and crash. So as soon as the engines begin to hum and before they begin that sullen scream, I close my eyes and I don't open them until after, for a moment, the plane and I have parted company. After that sickening lurch when we straighten out and I decide that, after all, we do have a pilot — then I open my eyes and look for the stewardess.

I opened my eyes, and Sam was laughing at me.

Laughter is comforting, though I would be hard put to say just why; that is, if it is nice laughter. Nice laughter makes rags and tatters of your terror. The stewardess wanted to know if we would care for anything. We certainly would.

We had an hour's wait in Chicago but at least it's better than it used to be when you had to cross the whole damn city to get to the Northern Pacific from the New York Central. And it is better to wait with someone than to wait alone. Alone, all you can do is clutch your bag and wish you hadn't read all the current magazines. Alone, you don't dare go to the ladies' room for fear they will call your flight and you won't hear it. So you have to wait until you are back on the plane, and that has disadvantages. I would like to warn all timid travelers not to look directly into the hopper.

There may be nothing there. It is a mistake, too, to lock the door. The lock may jam and there you will be, trapped and forgotten while everyone else is sliding down the escape chute. It is best to think of these contingencies before they happen.

Sam and I were not seated together out of O'Hare, but a nice little tummy-type of traveling salesman volunteered to change.

Flying invites disastrous intimacies. If you have only an hour to live, who cares? Though at that, planes are safer than trains, because there is so little room. For real trouble, commend me the drawing room with the night sliding by and an indulgent porter. Presently there is a grind of couplings and a long hoot. Lights flash by and the train groans and stops. Outside, there is Oshkosh or Mandan or Missoula and everything is brutally real again.

Sam and I did not become intimate. We exchanged a few shallow confidences. He knew that I was widowed. I learned he was divorced. By Denver I knew that he prefers filet mignon to coq au vin. We both like Burgundy and B. and B.

Then Jackson Hole was under us. That is a big country out there and I don't trust it. It seems unlikely that the plane is going to get over — and then between — those peaks and ridges, or that anyone has remembered to mow the landing field. The Grand Tetons do not really look like breasts; whoever named them must have been away from women for a long time. On one of those peaks there was a high wink of light and the stewardess told us it was all that was left of a Mormon mission plane. They never did reach the bodies. After she told us that we fastened our seat belts and she went behind the curtain, but not sufficiently. I could see her braced against the wall with her face in her hands; the copilot was comforting her. Then we were down. When she handed me my coat (it is cold in the Rockies in the fall) I asked her if she had known something that we didn't know. She said no, it wasn't that, it was only that she didn't like takeoffs and landings and it was probably time she transferred to a desk job. I took her word for it but didn't feel right until my feet hit the ground. I think she was probably telling me the truth, although I didn't stick around long enough to know whether or not she got on again. If she did, I hope she made it.

Airports are always out of town but in the West it seems farther because there is no point of reference. All those empty miles and all that sage. There were a couple of cars waiting that claimed to be cabs, but both of us were being met.

"By the way," I said. "What are you doing out here?"

I guess I thought he was going to settle a really big insurance claim or sell some tractors. But he was going to hunt elk. Hot damn!

I have to admit this made a lot of difference. Something vestigial in me likes the idea of men's going hunting. I like to think of them (as the song says) in the early morn drinking coffee from a can. And splashing cold creek water on their faces as the sweet smoke drifts from the campfire. And I like to picture them pursuing something, although I always hope that whatever it is it gets away. Not that I would like to do it myself, you understand. I just like to think about their doing it.

Already Sam was suffering a sea-change. The camaraderie of the flight was gone and he was shy again. There wasn't an ounce of laughter in him.

"Well," I said, "so goodbye."

Four nights later he called me up.

I have to explain about this friend of mine. She was one of the almost truly rich, and you know how they are. Her family canned something or other without which the American public could not get by from day to day. But naturally, she was suspicious. The almost truly rich urge experiences upon you which you could not otherwise afford, and if you accept they are very properly suspicious. Also, the rich never realize how much they cost us. It is true that at that time I could not afford a little shooting lodge in Wyoming, but then, I never wanted one. I never wanted those inlaid boots, either, nor the California pants or the beaten silver belt without which the pants could not be worn. And it was a long way to come to live in such dogged simplicity.

We slept in bunks because they were *echt*, and my friend was not one to take half measures. The thin lumpy mattresses were also *echt*. So was the food. So was the insolent help.

There is always a European at these house parties and the European is always critical. Even if the things he objects to are the very things that I object to, I want to be the one who does the criticizing. At least I had paid for my own fare, and I doubt if the Swiss did.

Among us sycophants there was one happy soul who spoke up. She was on the books as a secretary and she drew a salary but she was really paid for speaking up, and she was permitted and even encouraged to say things that the rest of us didn't say. That the coffee was bad and the cream had turned and that 6-12 wasn't keeping the mosquitoes away. My wealthy friend knew we were all thinking this, and she wanted to be in a position to fire anyone who said it aloud.

Four days of it was about enough for me.

There was a very grand dinner party planned for the fourth night. We had been eating a lot of mutton and a lot of beans because beans are also *echt*. But that night my almost truly wealthy friend was being visited by a truly wealthy friend whose family made the cans in which whatever my friend's family canned was canned. Therefore we were to have brook trout, which is not all it's cracked up to be: too many bones. The foreman's daughter, who was a cheerleader at the University of Utah and a home economics major, was going to serve the Châteauneuf du Pape.

Oh yes, there was a foreman and a few head of cattle. It looked better, and the annual loss was helpful with her income tax. The canner's daughter was to join us and, for local color, the Episcopal priest (very high), as well as a real cowboy, who had come second in the rodeo. We were to wear our Passamaquoddy moccasins and our silver squash-necklaces, neither of which is indigenous to Wyoming. After dinner we were to have café diable.

So I see why my wealthy friend was indignant when

I was summoned to the telephone, which was one convenience that we were not without. I was not supposed to know anyone else out there.

I knew his voice right away. He said, "I don't suppose you'd like to go to dinner?"

I balanced issues. If I ran out on her, my almost truly wealthy friend was not going to forgive. People forgive treachery and bad checks and even the misfortunes of their friends, but never simple rudeness. Nominally, the dinner was for me.

"No," Sam said. "Of course you wouldn't."

Men who are shy usually don't ask twice.

I said, "You bet your boots I would."

And it all turned out just as I predicted. She still spoke and we exchanged Christmas cards. But between us, it was never glad, confident morning again. And now we will neither speak nor exchange Christmas cards again.

On the other hand, since Sam hunts elk, I got a lot of wear out of the California pants.

20

LAST NIGHT Wes and I shared a cab on the way to the Merry-Go-Round; it was the first chance we had had all day to hold hands. Wes and I haven't been lovers for a long time but while it lasted it was very nice, and I don't think he has had anyone since me. This is not because he grieves for me but because it was never one of those wild affairs, just a good one, and he is an intelligent man and has other interests. But we are comfortable together and if I could talk to anyone I could talk to Wes, oddly enough because we are not involved with one another.

Last night he beat me to the punch.

He said, "What's wrong with Len?"

All along the mall the magnolias were rosy and behind the brownstones the sky was violet. The kids have worn paths everywhere and the pigeons have pecked bare patches, but there are dandelions in the grass.

"I don't know," I told him. "I think I know but I'm not sure."

If I had been sure I would have told him, because you can tell Wes things. That way, he's like Sam. Come to think of it, Wes is very much like Sam. They both survived their first and savage loves, and now we can all be quiet and hold hands. I could have told Wes what Len's trouble was if I had known what it was, and I could have told him what my trouble is if the moment had been right. But I don't know how I'm going to tell Sam.

I hate what's happening to Copley Square. Little old Trinity Church, so hideous and satisfying with its turrets and arches, is minimized and dwarfed by the frightening building that towers right behind it; the huge building can't possibly be made entirely of black glass but it looks as if it were, and the dark bulk of it with the little church squatting there below is curiously unsettling. The Prudential was bad enough, but at least the Prudential is your run-of-the-mill high-rise. This new one menaces like a Nazi, which tells you what generation I belong to.

But it is still nice, at the violet hour. Beyond the church the Plaza waited with its flags. Some misguided group caused the pedestrian mall to be paved with concrete and even the fountain cannot compensate, but the Public Library still watches gravely and the same brisk little old ladies and little tottering old men still pass upon the stairs. You can almost imagine a hansom cab carrying T. S. Eliot's aunt home with her reticule, her week's supply of instructive reading and her Boston *Evening Transcript*. The *Transcript* is long gone, alas, and even the *Herald-Traveler*, that upstart, is mourned this year. I had a moment of desire as piercing as a pin to say to hell with the Merry-Go-Round and to mount the steps to see how the Puvis de Chavannes murals are weathering. All around the library the great grave names still state in silence and simplicity how little most of us amount to.

There was a small snarl of traffic in front of the Plaza, so we were five minutes later than the others in disengaging from our cab. We parted on the best of terms; Wes has this thing with drivers and waiters and kids. Our driver was not one of the old traditionals with the tough veined Irish eyes, but a young man with a ponytail, a degree from Boston University and no opening in his field. He told us that the company was considering bulletproof glass between the driver and the passengers.

If an affair has been gentle and has died meekly, without recrimination or wounds, there is a pleasant thing left between participating partners. The excitement has gone but the intimacy has not, nor the real wish for one another's welfare. You know, beneath the clothing and the manners, where the other's scars are, and touch them not at all, or gently. Wes and I were still hand in hand when we stood at the door of the shadowy big room that houses the Merry-Go-Round.

Six are hard to seat. If there are more of you the waiters will usually put tables together, although reluctantly, like resentful housewives. On the Merry-Go-Round it can't be done; the best we could do was to get a table right behind the others. They had their first round of drinks already and one thing surprised me. Marta was not what I thought — indeed, she is a braw, brawny hand with the glass and the vermouth on the rocks was only until after business hours.

This explained a lot. Like most people who don't have to drink but like to, Len prefers company. And being merely male, of course he prefers company that is suave, well-dressed and conversant with the troubles and triumphs of his day. I think Gay makes a big mistake in cooking while he has his cocktails and reading until they go to bed. No matter how ardent she may be, a man likes a little conversation, too.

When I first heard of the Merry-Go-Round I imagined that you not only went around but up and down, and seated on some kind of modified horse. It is not like that, of course. Whoever had the bright idea in the first place was too bright to think that at that hour you can not only go around but up and down. You sit at tables and the round platform moves very slowly indeed — believe me, that's enough. The funny thing is that it's harder to get on than to get off, perhaps because when you get on you still have your caution about you. I suppose the charm of the Merry-Go-Round is some holdover from one's childhood — the minute one grasps a pole and swings aboard, one's gaiety quotient doubles.

I sipped slowly. A nice degree of Nirvana was what I was after, but I wanted no part of a hangover or at the most just the slightest one. More I could not afford. Wes and I had a lot of catching up to do and now,

islanded in the low light and with the music just loud
enough to mask our voices, it seemed a good time to do
it. He knew I would want to hear about Polly.

I first met Wes and Dorothea right after they had
heard.

Wes was a friend of Barry's; they had been to Deer-
field together and then to Brown, had separated in the
service, and then met again in business. Barry said,
"There isn't one damn thing to say, so don't say anything."

"Did you think I would?" I asked.

Wes at that time was the kind of looking man I have
always liked — tall, with a nice angular face and the
kind of heavy brows that are going to bristle fiercely if
he gets that old. Not that I noticed that first time; no
one could notice anything beyond the anguish in his
eyes. He was still so proud of her.

You see, Polly was never one of your lop-headed,
lolling retardeds. She was a beautiful child and from the
beginning had never shown any of those signs you're
supposed to look for — she pulled herself up in her crib
when she was supposed to and crawled when she was
supposed to and walked early . . . no, ran. In those days
we didn't know about urinalysis for the newly born;
the little body was perfect and the small head exquisitely
proportioned and she was so active. Too active. But in
those days we didn't know about autistic children, either.

Much later, when he could talk about it, I asked Wes
what had first worried them. For a long time, nothing.
Many children are slow to talk. But Polly never met

their eyes and never was engaged in anything. She was all laughter and all motion and none of it was remotely directed. At three, she was not toilet trained. For a long time Dorothea resisted bitterly any thought of an evaluation, but Wes lay awake long worrying about the little body that beat in his arms like a bird.

That day, if I hadn't known I wouldn't have guessed. Overexcited, I might have thought; this will end in tears. Dorothea never looked in the child's direction. She sat in a lawn chair with a lemonade in her hand and her pretty, drawn face showed her strain. But she had removed herself from the problem. It was Wes who had fenced the yard and who watched that elf-baby, that quicksilver child who could flutter into danger random as a butterfly, that girl-child with the wild, lovely eyes behind which something, simply, had been left out. Every doctor said she would never be any different.

Neither would Dorothea.

I know that one person can never say how another person should take tragedy, but I don't think that Dorothea took it well. I suppose those grey distant eyes might well ask, how would I know? And she would have a point. But I've had my own losses, and one thing I know — if you sulk your life away, who has won?

I thought (and Barry thought so too) that it was hard on Wes. She wouldn't keep the child at home, though I suppose you can't fault her there; she had the very best advice. She wouldn't visit her at the expensive home. She wouldn't have another child though every doctor said it would not happen again. And just to be sure it didn't happen again — you're right — she wouldn't. All this time Wes just worked harder and was cheerful, which is not the same thing as being happy.

Last night I asked to see Polly's latest picture; Wes always carries one. He goes to see her every month, although she doesn't recognize him. She is sixteen now and still beautiful. They dress her modishly at that place and in the background you see sandpiles and swings. She is still not toilet trained.

When you glance up from the Merry-Go-Round the room is never where you expect it to be, which is reasonable. Even in a stationary bar it is hard to keep track of the groups that come and go and to remember where the doors are. But the drinks must have been getting to me, because just then I saw something at the next table that was not reasonable at all, and yet it did not occur to me to mention it. It was a small thing — just that upon that table there was a glass that flamed as if it were on fire. It was a pretty thing, though unaccountable, and I might have drawn it to Wes's attention except that just then he reached across the table and took my hand.

"How is it with you?" he asked.

I looked right back into his good tired eyes under the brier-patch brows and said "I'm all right, Jack." Because at that moment, I was.

Behind me I could hear Walter's voice raised in what I assume was unaccustomed mirth. And then he swung around and tapped my shoulder. His glasses had slipped a little and those great unsophisticated eyes were beaming. "Let's have another one," he said. "I want to buy everyone another one. Let's drink to the future and the past."

"That's all right with me," Wes said.

When the waiter came, he had a third glass on his tray. He rubbed its base firmly on the table and by God, it lighted.

"Very pretty," Wes said. "But why?"

"Search me," the waiter said. "Some people get a kick out of it."

I found that I had reached my confidential stage. "The last time I was here," I told the waiter, "I was on my honeymoon."

He said, "A lot of folks tell us that." Then he said proudly, "I been here myself for twenty years." I looked with respect at the man who had been at the Copley for twenty years. "Hell," he said, "I been a Southie all my life. Why, I remember Curley. But the old town isn't what it was," he said.

I wondered what he minded most: the blacks, the Puerto Ricans, the assertive young, the traffic, the crime rate, the airport . . .

"What's the worst change?" I asked.

"The Sox used to be a good ball team," he said. "And the Braves were even better. Excuse me, please."

Wes and I smiled together. We always have enjoyed that kind of small exchange; unlike Len, who is always affable, which is not the same thing as being friendly. Len likes the idea of waiters, but is not drawn to them as individuals. Gay is always vaguely apologetic with them, as if there were something not quite right about her being there or else their being there.

Wes said, "What is he like — Sam?"

"Oh . . ." I was thinking, yes, he is quite a lot like you, Wes. Tender. Generous. Kindly. Concerned. Then why did I leave you and marry him? Because he was free to marry me. On the whole, I prefer being married; it is neater and eliminates all the cat-and-mouse busy-ness that is fun to think about but not much fun to act out. I got tired of the stolen hour, the stolen night, the disguised telephone message, the accommodation address. I wanted to wake up with someone warm beside me who would kiss me before my teeth were brushed.

And I got tired of always being at my best. It made me feel that the woman who met you at restaurants, at motels, out of town, didn't exist or at least was a different woman. Get her, I would think — always scented and tranquil and attentive — who does she think she's kidding? Besides, you said a small thing once and after you said it nothing was the same. You said, "It's only fair to tell you. I'll never leave Dorothea."

Who asked you to? We were just playing, weren't we? I felt rubbed and injured because you felt that perhaps I wasn't just playing. It diminished your value to me.

Just thinking about it I got angry and took a large swallow of my drink. I had promised myself an evening without anger or melancholy, or fear. And I was suddenly lonely for Sam because of thinking about him, which was another thing I had promised myself I would not do last night. You know those good marriages — there are some — where both partners have survived being in love and have achieved comfort and habit and are courteously content? That's what we have. We spent our tantrums, our lacerations and our ecstasies on other people. It's not all that good, being in love: look at Gay. It's not even altogether seemly, at our age. All that panting and trembling.

But if that is what I think — and it is what I think — why wouldn't I take Sam's call? Why didn't I get up right that moment and find a phone booth, which is what Len was doing? He paused briefly to say he'd be right back, and then half-stumbled from the revolving bar and caught his balance again while we swirled slowly, and gracefully I'm sure, away from him.

The reason I wasn't going to talk to Sam was that he deserved last night. One more night without terror. At least I think that was the reason. I hope so.

Damn Wes's question.

But then I didn't have to think about it anymore because Gay provided me with a diversion, an uncharacteristic and disquieting one that brought me closer to the edge of sobriety than I wished to be.

What happened was that first, Gay raised her voice. Now, this is a thing I have never known to happen before, with a single exception. Gay raised her voice to call a child if — and only if — the child was in danger or if it was Gay's opinion that the child was in danger. Otherwise, never. Grandmother had many maxims about what became and did not become a lady. What they boiled down to was that a lady does not in any way attract attention to herself.

Therefore a small lady does not chew gum nor eat on the street (including ice-cream cones) nor ever, ever lean against a building. Later, a lady rises when anyone older enters a room. She is considerate of her inferiors and she does not admit to pain or inflict her personal discomforts upon others. And all this had its practical and rewarding side; Grandmother liked to quote, "A brave heart and a courteous tongue will carry you far through the jungle, manling."

I don't know, it still doesn't seem like a bad idea, although I suppose today the whole concept of a lady is as dead as the dodo. Anyway, what you ended up with is a person relatively easy to live with whose clothing is never noticed.

My aunt had her own notions too, but they were easily summed up: a lady's accessories match.

So I was startled when I heard Gay's voice, sharp and clear over the muted music and the rain-drum of other people's conversation. She was on her feet. Her back was turned to me, but I could tell that she was angry. Her head was high, her shoulders rigid, and I didn't have to see her face to know her nostrils flared.

Then it all happened so quickly that I was left struggling to my feet, which wasn't easy because first I had to grope for one shoe which I had eased off, the way a person will. Gay, swinging the straw carryall, was well ahead of me and striding easily through the crowded room, circling the tables with a graceful swing of her hips that anxious as I was, I had to notice and admire. She pushed through a door and disappeared and I bolted after her and found her marching through the kitchens, oblivious to the interest of the pastry cooks and the salad men. It was a strange place to catch up with a friend in need of being caught up with. But I do have presence of mind.

"We're looking for the ladies' room," I said. "Could you direct us?"

They could, and did.

Thank God this one was empty, even of a maid. Gay said with a phrase that made me thoughtful, since I should have assumed it went out with the last lady: "I've never been so insulted in all my life."

The first thing I did was to get some cold water on Gay's face and — remembering she was a lady — on her wrists, which I think used to be considered calming. By the time she was dry she was laughing, though with more rue than amusement. And it was sort of funny.

What had happened was that Walter had been expounding more loudly and with more enthusiasm than Gay considered appropriate to a public place. And then the waiter came.

Gay said, "He rubbed a glass on the table — honestly he did — as if it were some kind of signal."

I said, "It's supposed to light up."

"Well, it didn't," she said. "And *then* he said, 'I'm sorry — this table is out of order.' "

She breathed deeply, with the offended majesty of one who had never in all her life been out of order.

"Just the same," I said, "that isn't what made you mad."

My friend is honest. She is also bright. She was silent for a moment and then she said, "No, that wasn't it, was it."

Gay and I read psychology together before it became as usual as rain and before every twelfth grader could explain the neuroses of his friends and parents. We didn't take the course because we didn't have the time and because the man who taught it was a fool and besides, he made us sad. We were at some kind of banquet once and his wife related that on her wedding night she waked to find she had hurled her new golden ring across the room. We were never sure whether the wife was simpleminded or just vindictive.

Nowadays everyone knows a little something about the mind, although it doesn't seem to have helped as much as one could wish. But when we were undergraduates, having read even lightly in the field made us feel more profound than other people. We played fair, too, and ploughed through a whole dullard of a text on normal behavior — though none of it seems more than fairly normal — before we permitted ourselves the eccentric. I still think a lot of it is useful. Long after one has forgotten the man who was in love with his mother's shoelace, it is wise to remember that the masks we wear are really intended to deceive ourselves.

So now Gay said, "No, that's not what made me angry, is it."

Friendship is better based on the things you don't say than the things you do. But anyway, I said it. "She shouldn't have come along. What does she think she's accomplishing?"

My friend rejected this. "You're wrong," she said. "Of course she's mad about him — Len's a very attractive man." She spoke as if he were someone she had often admired, if only from a distance. Then she said,

"Marta's not the first woman who's been mad about him."

That gave me quite a turn, or would have if it wasn't all so long ago. And Gay spoke with the terrible ease of a woman whose man still goes to bed with her. I could have told her something about that, but then, I've been around more than she has. I remember once when my ardent partner threw his arm across me and in sleep, spoke another name.

"I do dislike her," Gay said, "and she does make me mad. But that's because she's presumptuous. And she does encourage him in silly habits."

She didn't explain what she meant by silly habits, but I assume she meant the little drinking sessions after office hours.

"Beyond that," Gay said, "she's harmless."

I wasn't at all sure Marta was harmless. You take a man with a natural bent for pleasure and a deep-seated worry — whoever provides the escape route may not be harmful, but she certainly holds the potential for harm.

However, I groped for my comb. My first impulse may have been to prove myself correct; that's understandable, although not pretty. But I'm not one to tell my best friend what she doesn't want to know on the debatable grounds that she damn well ought to know. If Gay hadn't followed, like hounds and hares, the shabby clues I thought that I had followed, it was no act of friendship to lead her to the warren I had reached, and anyway, to descend to a discussion of where Len keeps his razor and his extra shirt is honestly below me.

Besides, the wife who doesn't know is in the best position. Alas, we have all reached the age when we are like to be off with the gypsies, and if Len is tempted, Gay's best protection is her appalling innocence.

So instead, I told her what the waiter had really meant.

21

GAY BLUSHED a deep, unbecoming rose.

I tried to make a funny out of it; I spread my fingers over my face and peered between them, a fool's gesture that did not amuse her.

She said, "Did I ever tell you how much that annoys me?"

Well no, she hadn't. On the other hand, I didn't realize I had done it all that often. Sam thinks it's kind of cute.

And then because my friend is formidably straightforward, we got to the kernel of it. I have never been so convinced as she is that honesty is a virtue. So often it is rude.

"I *hate* drinking," she said. "I absolutely hate drinking. Can you imagine my making such a fool mistake if I weren't drinking?"

Well, no. Although I myself would not dignify Dubonnet as drink. Gay was quivering with defense, and I knew what she would rather be doing than standing in a public toilet quivering. She would rather be home with an adequate book — if she didn't have an adequate one, an inadequate one would do. She would prefer to be reading over her coffee and over her dishes and in her bath, and then she would like to look in on John and to be sure that what he was reading was adequate. Then she would wait for Len, open-armed in the darkness. But if you are a troubled man, it's a long time between dinner and bed.

I asked, "What's wrong between you two?"

She answered promptly. "We are a bit divided over Charley. Len condemns Charley and everything he does. He'd do better to look at his own way of life."

I thought my friend was wrong. I thought Len didn't condemn anyone. But he was terrified. Oh, he loves Gay and he loves John and a little bit, he loves me and he is probably rather fond of Marta, but at the moment his whole being was scarified by his fear for Charley.

When you have been friends for a long, long time, it is not always easy to distinguish what you have seen yourself from what the other has told you. My aunt always said I couldn't remember her spanking me because I drew the postman and put his dingle in, but I think I remember. I think I remember the satisfying pencil strokes and how proud I was of my drawing, though it was just a stick-man — with a difference. My aunt remembered the drawing but denied, flushing, that she would have punished me. And by the way, how did I know about the dingle? Could it have been before my father died? That would have made me very young indeed, and perhaps I have been unjust. Perhaps nobody spanked me. Perhaps I added the spanking myself when I grew old enough to know that one does not draw dingles.

I remember a lot about Charley's childhood because (I suppose) I battened on Gay's life, having lost my own. I could swear I was there that day but perhaps I wasn't, come to think of it.

It all started as a simple locking of antlers. Len said that Charley was to do something or not to do something: that's immaterial. Charley said that he wouldn't.

Len said by God he would.

Charley said no.

Gay went away into the kitchen and began to count the silver with her hands trembling slightly. If I wasn't there, how would I remember that her hands were trembling? She kept losing count. She must have been polishing the silver to begin with, because it is not the sort of thing one would elect to do suddenly, in the middle of a battle *royale*. But I'm not even sure of that because Gay is meticulous and polishes her silver quite a lot and perhaps I am imagining that is what she was doing. But unless I was there, how do I know that it was all there, including the commemorative spoons her mother had brought back from Zurich and from Amsterdam? Gay does her silver with a book propped up (she uses a sponge to hold the pages open; I like a spatula, myself) so she worries, afterward. It is so easy to send a spoon scuttling into the garbage with the orange rinds and the steak fat.

Charley said no.

Len said, oh yes you will, and he took off his belt.

I suppose Len felt the boy had to be made to render unto Caesar. I suppose Charley felt he was fighting for his life.

There are all kinds of strappings. We are told that some of them are sadistic and that the battered child is battered for the parent's pleasure or release, and I suppose that is so, ugly though it is to contemplate. But I think most strappings are motivated by a parent's desperate recognition that if a child will not conform, the world has waiting a much heavier lash.

If the young man will not render unto Caesar, how shall he survive?

And the child desperately resists, because in a world of straps and lashes, how else can he survive?

They fought up and down the stairs while Gay lost track of the demitasse spoons, those delicate objects that enchant small girls but are easy to lose track of because we never use them anymore and who is to be sure if we started with ten or twelve? Gay said (and this I do remember) that she didn't interfere, not so much because it was drummed into our generation that to interfere with the mate's discipline is the sin against the domestic Holy Ghost but because she didn't think it was so much a matter of discipline as of males' strife, and when males are striving, women are better off counting spoons.

Certainly this is unfair. It is also true.

Every woman knows the sounds of her own house, and Gay didn't have to be watching to know when they lurched against the banisters or when the strap missed Charley's bare legs and slapped that loose corner of the new wallpaper. She heard when Charley retreated under his bed — his room was right above the kitchen — and she heard the scuttling sound of Len on his stomach trying to reach an ankle or a wrist and the wail when he got the child cornered and the curse when the child broke loose and then the feet thundering down the stairs again.

The door to the basement opened and slammed and the crash and thrash continued and then stopped abruptly. Then Gay was frightened, because the railing on those stairs was frail and the floor below cement, and so she waited with the demitasse spoons clicking like castenets until from above she heard John rock his crib and begin to chatter with his teddy bear. Then she opened the basement door.

Len and Charley were sitting halfway down with their arms around one another, clutched as if each were drowning. They were both crying.

"I hope you're both satisfied," Gay said. "You woke the baby."

The last time that I saw those little spoons was at a coffee for the League of Women Voters in which, at the time, Gay was trying to embroil me. I was helping her do up, and after we had clucked over the lipstick on the napkins she ran the hot water and watched severely as the steam and suds combatted.

Then she said, "Listen, will you check the spoons? There should be twelve."

Do you suppose that is when she told me all about it?

22

And suddenly I was frightened, too. Gut-frightened.

"Drugs?" I asked.

"Heavens, no." She hesitated. "I don't know," she said. "I honestly don't know. You see, he doesn't keep in touch." With a paper towel she scrubbed her old lipstick off and then leaned to the mirror and drew a new, perfect mouth. "They're all alike these days," she said.

Oh, no they aren't. Not any more than we were all alike.

"The thing is," my friend said, "Len lets it distort his thinking. For goodness' sake, we had our own convictions but we learned to live with them. Charley will, too."

Maybe. One thing I know — if these kids think the King is wrong, there's no America for them to go to. There is no wilderness for them to conquer unless they make their own wilderness and if they do, I hope to God they can conquer it.

Another thing I know. If the man you love is

troubled and afraid, you'd better find some way to take his hand. Or someone else will.

"I know what you're thinking," Gay said, though for once she was wrong. She met my eyes in the cold silver of the mirror. "But Charley is my son, too."

I fashioned my own mouth. I thought that Gay was partly right and partly wrong, but then, I always think everyone is both right and wrong and as Sam points out, the end of that is paralysis. But damn it, I am not my sister's keeper.

We looked better when we left the ladies' room but I was feeling worse and was quite unreasonably impatient with my friend. If I didn't choose to tell her — and I didn't choose to tell — there was no way she could know that the throbbing and pressure had begun again that is something more than distress and something less than pain. I needed gin.

The others were waiting in the lobby but Len wasn't with them; he was on the phone again. Gay spoke in a low tone and a quiet temper. "He doesn't trust John, now. Sometimes I think . . ."

That Len had driven Charley away? I saw that underneath that cool demeanor, Gay was frightened too. Charley is very much Gay's son. I saw that clearly one day before John was born.

Perhaps because she had lost the little girl, all during that pregnancy Gay walked as if she were carrying a chalice. I watched her walking that way one day on the beach. I was overnighting with them; it was the first summer that they rented the house in Gloucester that they later bought. Len was going to be late and we had been swimming, the three of us. Charley was ten.

It was a bright day, but rough; the water was smacking in the harbor and Gay spent most of her time on the sand wrapped in a villainous old toweling robe because she burns. Charley and I were good friends that year. Boys are nice at ten. They are old enough to talk to and some of the things they say are quite interesting. And they haven't yet made the sad discovery of themselves and drawn apart, appalled and enchanted. He already swam better than I; to keep up with him through that choppy dark blue water took every ounce of strength I had and I had an uncomfortable feeling that if anyone's safety was being watched out for, it wasn't Charley's. When I pleaded the cold he came out docilely, his skinny shoulders slick with salt water and trembling, his lips just a little blue, the way their lips get. He raced the length of the beach and came back dry and rosy through his tan and with the salt dried on his shoulders like a powder. I knew enough not to brush it off.

"It's late," Gay said. "Let's go."

There was a long stairway of grey sun-and-rain-scoured wood (you had to watch for splinters) that led from that beach to the parking lot. Charley sped up it like a monkey and I wasn't far behind. At the top I paused, and because after the sand and water it is always depressing to see the cars flashing in the sun in rows, each with its bit of pasteboard saying its owner was empowered to come to that beach and so many of them with rabbit tails dangling over the steering wheel or plastic Christs and Virgins on the dashboard that bobbed sullenly when the car was in motion, I turned my back on them and looked back to where the clean water and the clean sand met. I don't suppose it was clean, even then, but it *looked* clean. A lot of what you don't know won't hurt you.

Below us Gay was trudging through the sand. We had been rather good about bringing the blanket and the thermos bottle and the magazines, so she carried nothing but her own proud, lonely burden. She stopped at the bottom of the steps and then, before she began to climb, she gathered the terrible old robe behind her knees and bunched its folds under her stomach in the immemorial, antique gesture of women climbing stairs, and lifted her face to us. At that moment, my friend was not even pretty. Her face was gaunt, her bright hair dulled and tousled. It didn't matter. Her eyes were calm and clear and she held her head like a dancer. She held the robe in one hand and with the other, reached for the railing.

That's what I saw. I don't know what Charley saw. It's been a long time since boys of ten haven't known everything there is to know. Well, almost everything. I only know what he did. He was back down those steps in a flash and she waited for him. When he reached her he held his hand out to her and my friend took it.

And then she smiled at him. I saw her.

Ah, I thought. So that is what it is to have a son.

Len didn't look like a father who didn't trust his young. He looked like a man who for some reason, is apprehensive. I wondered uneasily if Charley had been in touch.

Marta was terribly at ease. I felt she had rather enjoyed our small excitement and the opportunity it afforded her to be circumspect and useful. She had gathered up the cigarettes Len had left behind and she had paid his portion of the bill. She had also found and brought along a very nice handkerchief of Gay's which had been jettisoned in the speed of her departure.

Gay said a spiteful thing. She said, "Isn't that what assistants are supposed to do — assist?" And then, having made an enemy of her enemy, she gathered herself together and asked lightly, "Is John all right?" Which reminded everyone of who everyone was and belonged to. So we left rather regally. After small furors, one does like to depart with dignity. No one could have been more dignified than the six of us, waiting in front of the Copley for a cab.

While we waited, Wes looked at me closer than I like to be looked at.

"Are you OK?" he asked.

"What's it to you?" I said.

That wasn't very nice. He hadn't even known I was angry at the time he said that about Dorothea, let alone that I was remembering it last night. But as a matter of fact, I wasn't feeling very well. It is starting just the way it did last time. They say it is all in my favor that I didn't wait at all this time, but of course I did hope there wasn't going to be this time.

However, in my purse I had the wherewithal to make

me feel much better and I'm not talking about pills. Any fool knows you don't mix pills and liquor, not until you mean to. I had the prescription filled, of course, but I hadn't used any except for that one night when I told Sam I'd better go back to Boston. I didn't even take one the next day while I tried to talk him out of coming with me.

"Why not?" he kept asking. "Why?"

So finally I told him why. "I don't want you," I said. I've said a lot of mean things in my time.

What I had in my purse was my lovely flask. I don't know why more people don't use them all the time, but I suppose it's because you can't get them any more, anyway not like this one. You can find any number fitted for picnic baskets, and last year I saw one advertised in the *New Yorker* that was guaranteed not to break while your airplane luggage is thrown around the way your airplane luggage is always thrown around. But you don't see any more like mine — it is thin as a wafer and made of beaten silver and it is slightly curved on one side to fit a hip and my father's initials are on it. I kept it because I like to have the tangible proof that he had fun before he died. You know? But then later on I knew someone who always carried a shot in her purse in an aspirin bottle and I thought, why not? Believe me, there are times when it is wise.

Right then it seemed wise. And as I looked at Len's taut face I decided it would be wise for him, too, so I maneuvered the two of us into one cab and let the others tag along the best they could. I have always tried to be reasonably honest with myself; it's more interesting that way. I really was concerned about Len's comfort. But it also did seem to me that he was at a very dangerous stage and that the evening was in the balance. Whatever John had reported had not pleased him and he was only one step away from sobriety, which could well mean a fast dinner, a black coffee and an early bedtime for all of us: that is the way Len is. Which did not suit my plans at all. Not that I had considered any attractive wickedness; it was just that I didn't want last night to end. Not ever.

This taxi driver was one of a different breed. He was so old, frail, and resentful of anyone who was not that I didn't know whether I dared take out my flask or not. He might very well draw up to the curb and say, "Well, that did it. Out."

So I was cautious as I eased my treasure forth and pleased to see that Len, at least, was not offended. In fact, he was almost not offended enough. "Just a minute," I said. "That only holds two drinks, you know." He parted with it.

The use of alcohol requires discretion, and years of assiduous practice teaches one how to maintain that tightrope equilibrium without toppling either into drunkenness or sobriety. But useful as my flask is, it is not ideal for us gin drinkers. Warm gin, even laced with warm vermouth, is honestly not very palatable. So whiskey it has to be, no matter what went before it or what will follow. Len didn't seem to mind.

It didn't seem to cheer him up much, either, and I

had an uneasy moment when I wondered if I had over-looked an important item in the planning of such an evening, which is the initial mood of those who are to partake. You can have a bad trip on alcohol, too.

"You haven't been the same since you talked to John," I complained. "Is he sniffing glue?"

He looked at me with real, if temporary, hatred. "Very funny," he said.

"Hey, listen," I said, "What's eating on you?"

At the moment we were passing the very furrier where my aunt bought me that ratty muskrat coat on sale. Not that I knew it was ratty then, but as I think of it, it was a pretty bad coat. It had a sort of round low collar that left your throat open to every wind and from the first, the hairs were coming out. My aunt was a generous person and meant well; it was just that she had a limited income and rotten taste. And then, briefly, we stopped in traffic in front of Mark Cross, where we used to yearn over all the soft, lovely, expensive leather. I did buy a key-case there once. It wasn't much of a present, but my aunt liked the small box it came in. It said "Mark Cross."

Last night a couple of kids were yearning into those same windows; I have to admit not the most attractive of their kind. There's something about bare feet in the city that makes you think of dogs and spittle, and fannies patched with hands and hearts lack a certain *je ne sais quoi*. But they were holding hands and I thought they were kind of cute.

Len said, "What's eating me? *Them!*" And there was

so much venom in his voice that I said the very thing that everyone always says — I said, "That doesn't sound like you."

Old Gruffanuff's shoulders had snapped straight. He said, "You said a mouthful, mister."

We didn't say any more until he let us out at the corner of Tremont and Winter streets. The Common was blue now and the dancers gone; above the walks the streetlights bloomed like tall white dandelions and the light lay in dusty strips on the worn grass. On the subway kiosk someone had painted STOP THE BOMBING — the brush had dripped. I thought of all the tunnels spoking out down there and of the great caverns of the underground garage, and I felt we stood on a soiled shallow shell that would crack at any moment and drop us all: Len, me, that bearded black, the woman muttering to herself and the one who was walking her threadbare cat, and the young man with one earring and a sash.

Len said, "I don't want Gay to know. But Ottawa's been calling. I've got the number but I haven't been able to get through."

"Charley?" I asked.

"I assume so," Len said bitterly.

And whee — here it all came, what's grabbing him, what's got him by the short hairs, what's lining his eyes and souring his nice mouth and what might very well spoil my party: they are a different tribe by choice, by willfulness, by God sometimes by force. Look at their tribal scars and ceremonial clothes. The different tribe is the enemy tribe and we are the different tribe and the enemy. They invade our territory, they use our space. Our tribe is driven from the Common, shouldered from the sidewalks, pushed to our cars, to our homes (if we're lucky); to our offices.

"To the Ritz," I suggested.

Yes, to the Ritz.

They refuse our envoys and our messengers. They will not be advised nor accept our solace nor our help. Up yours, they say. What's more, their infection is pandemic: how does he know that John will not succumb? Already he wears his hair long; Gay permits it. They will not listen to the council, they run with the Bandar-log — what's going to happen to them?

"*What's going to happen to them?*" Len cried.

He means, what's going to happen to Charley?

"What's going to happen?" Len cried with the cry of all fathers at all times: rage, love, and pity.

A breeze sent a crumpled cigarette package scuttling into the gutter by our feet. Across the street, caught in the thinning blades of grass, gum wrappers blossomed. I shut my eyes against the blinking of the neon tubes and told myself that if the other cab came before I had counted fifteen, the evening would still end well. I often do this. If *this* happens, *that* will follow. It often works out this way. Try it and see.

Everything in Boston is one-way. To get by cab from Bolyston Street to Tremont you have to turn left on Charles and right on Beacon and right again at the Park Street Church on the "Brimstone Corner," and one-way or not, you can be held up. I opened my eyes and all the cabs were moving briskly, but none of them were inching over toward us. I probably hadn't counted right. No, that's the living truth; I hadn't stipulated how quickly I would count and anyone knows you should count by seconds and that to count by seconds you have to say "one steam engine, two steam engine" between counts, which I hadn't done. So I got to count again. Whatever this Power is that I woo with my stratagems, it is often fair.

"Charley never writes," Len said more quietly. "We don't know where he's living or who he's living with or how he makes his living if he makes a living. Or if he's in trouble with the police. But something's wrong, for him to call. So don't tell Gay."

"I won't," I promised. Of course I wouldn't tell Gay.

The other cab pulled up and the rest of us piled out, but whether it was going to be all right or not I didn't know, because I had lost count again.

"It's their own fault," Len said, not meaning our friends but a clutch of youngsters passing with vacant laughter. "The whole damn generation."

Not so, Len, and you know it.

No one is at fault for anything: didn't we all agree about this years ago? We are grains of sand in an hourglass. And while it is true that one grain has to move (or maybe just one molecule within that grain) and nudge his neighbor before the process starts that moves us from our beginning to our end, that grain cannot be said to be at fault. We must believe this. If it is not true we admit responsibility, and that is unacceptable. Start with the notion of responsibility and you end entertaining the idea of hell.

Wholesome woman that I am and because I see so clearly that it is guilt that makes us dangerous to one another, I feel we must retreat from guilt. Why do you think St. Simeon Stylites retreated to that pillar?

Therefore, to prove that I myself am guiltless as the Virgin and need not be unkind to anyone, I reached my hand to Gay who had stumbled in her thin-strapped sandals, smiled warmly at Walter with his fame and fortune clutched beneath his arm, and snuggled my hand winningly into Wes's. Guilty? *Me?*

True, I betrayed my friend, but only once and that was a long time ago. True, I have played the wanton from time to time and chambered here and there. And laughed at my aunt, who was always so afraid that someone was going to laugh. And been unkind to Sam, who has been kind to me.

And I did give Charley that two hundred dollars.

"Alibi Ike," my aunt used to say. My only alibi is that he was distraught, and I was there.

23

THIS HAPPENED the year before Charley beat the draft and the year after he had — metaphorically speaking — cursed his mother. Of course he never cursed Gay: he never said a rude thing to her in his life. We were all pleased when he turned against Rimbaud; we should not have been so pleased when he deserted Wittgenstein. Nor was I a bit disturbed when Gay wrote that (as far as she could see) he had given up drinking. I guess I assumed he was on pot which, as everyone knows, is an innocent and wholesome substance, though it may get you in some trouble with the fuzz.

What I did not consider (neither did his parents) was that Charley had fallen prey to the most dangerous stimulant of all, the one that attacks at all ages but is most virulent when the flesh is neat on the bone and the blood fast and fresh: love.

That time I had nothing to hide and everyone knew I was in town. I didn't stay with Gay and Len because I was traveling with Sam although I wasn't registered with him. Gay wasn't offended because we were to wed, just as soon as his children got used to me. They missed their mother.

I had seen Charley at the big house in Cambridge but hadn't had much of a chance to talk to him. He never says much when he is around his parents, but I understand from those who have had parents that that is not unusual. He looked quite neat. That is, he wore a jacket, although it didn't fit him, being too short in the sleeves and oddly enough, too broad across the shoulders. He even wore a tie of sorts, though you could see his shirt wasn't buttoned under it. He left right after dinner. This surprised none of us; we are not so old that we don't all remember how you have to leave right after dinner. I thought Len behaved very well. He made no fatuous fatherly remarks but only said, "It's good to see you," and let it go at that.

Naturally I was pleased and more than a bit relieved when Charley called next day from the lobby and asked to come up. That last meeting hadn't been what you'd call a whale of a success. When they grow up, things change. You knew a small person and the tall person is a different person; negotiations have to start again, and amnesties.

When Charley comes into a room, you know it. For weal or woe, he is a forceful boy. The air sort of moves in front of him; he displaces atmosphere. Because of that and because I wasn't expecting her, it was a moment before I realized the girl.

She was a slim little thing who burned like a flame. I don't know if you'd call her a pretty girl and I thought she looked frail, but you could have warmed your hands before that radiance. She wore a belted dress and real shoes with little heels. Sure, I think it was to impress me: what's wrong with that? Her manners were graceful as a minuet. I suspect that like the shoes, they were put on to please, but the point is that she had them to put on. If you ask me, there's a lot too much loose talk about sincerity. I go for deference and courtesy and girls who know how to get in and out of rooms.

Charley said, "This is Mary Beth. She's at Regis."

Of course. You can't beat the nuns for getting in and out of rooms.

Charley was proud of her. "She's on full scholarship," he said.

She couldn't have been nineteen. Another thing I liked — she loved him (she shone with love) but she wasn't taken in. When he spoke she listened and her wide sweet Irish mouth was serious, but her eyes laughed.

What do you offer a pair of kids in love?

"Coffee, tea, milk?" I asked, "or how about a belt of bourbon?"

She passed that test, too. "I'd like a drink," she said. So I fixed three, two rather pale and one rather dark.

We spent a very pleasant half an hour. I wasn't sure whether he was selling her to me or me to her, but he paraded what was best of both of us. One thing did puzzle me. I don't think Gay and Len knew about her. I suppose it was because of the natural secrecy of young men and their blind drive toward autonomy. There couldn't be any other reason. Gay would have loved Mary Beth.

But at that age, alas, they are not autonomous.

Like all convent-reared girls she was modest (I don't mean physically — she showed her pretty legs) but she didn't want to say much about the scholarship except that she had always liked languages. I did learn a few things about her. Her family summered at Nantucket and she had two sisters and one brother. All the girls went to the Academy of the Sacred Heart, which is in Wellesley — you can see it from the bus. Then all the girls went to Regis. The brother was at Holy Cross. One uncle was a Jesuit and one a canon.

Charley was nervous. He smoked incessantly and didn't hit the ashtray often. And he wasn't really interested in his drink but did a lot of rattling of ice.

Then he said, "Mary Beth. Wait for me in the lobby."

When the door closed behind her he said, "Well, she's pregnant."

Why me?

Oh, you know why. Because I had a trick up my sleeve.

I didn't even bother with the banalities, such as why they didn't tell their families. Because he wasn't telling his family anything that year, and because her parents would have wanted her to have the child. I only asked two questions, because they were the only ones I thought important. The first was why they didn't just get married.

"Because we don't want it," he said. "Not this one."

I was to understand that this was no sexual collision, but a mating for life. But he would probably have to go into the damned army and she wanted at least her master's. Besides, it was safe and even legal now and she had already found a doctor who had referred her to a doctor in New York. The doctor in New York thought it was early enough for the vacuum, but if that didn't do the trick it was just a matter of a D and C and she could be gone for a weekend and right back in time for finals.

Charley was white-knuckled. He hated every moment of this. "It isn't that we don't want kids," he said. "It's more that she just doesn't want this one."

They had sold everything they had to sell, both bicycles and his tape recorder and their typewriters.

So I asked the second important question. I said, "How much do you need?"

Why did I do it? Because I was proud to be the one he asked. Because I was willing to bind him with hoops of gratitude. Because when Charley went out with me, nobody knew that he was not my son.

So I got my checkbook out and added a bit to what he'd asked because you never know when something will come up. I numbered the check and signed it with a flourish and handed to my godson his wicked godmother's gift.

And I have cursed the day.

Because against all the laws of medicine, statistics and probability, she died.

She did, she died. On the third day her fever rocketed, and by the time her roommate caught on and the housemother got her to the hospital, she had suffered irreversible vascular collapse.

The doctor who spoke to us was very kind. He said it was nobody's fault. He said it happens more often than any of us know. He said it doesn't show up in the figures because the girls are out of state and home before they die. He told us that under the most controlled conditions, for the first sixty hours after instrumentation, infection can occur.

He said he was sorry: such a lovely girl.

The death certificate said that Mary Beth died of septic shock.

Nobody's fault. Oh, sure. My aunt would have said, tell it to the Marines.

On the whole, Mary Beth's family behaved fairly well. From their point of view she was a murderess and a suicide, and Charley only an accesory before the fact. They were savage enough to insist on meeting him, but not enough to insist on meeting Len and Gay.

So I don't think they ever knew about it — Len and Gay. I certainly didn't tell them, though I think that was a mistake. It was a very personal matter and I felt that it was up to Charley to make that confidence. I don't think he did. Gay wouldn't keep anything of that moment from me. Why did I keep it from her? Because I am more devious than she is and more cowardly.

But it was a mistake.

They have a right to know why Charley runs. He isn't running from their plans or from their love. He runs from heartbreak.

I wonder how many of them are running from heartbreak.

Charley has never been in touch with me since, not in any way. How could he?

But grief, like guilt, corrupts; it makes us cruel. I hope nobody grieves for me, or not excessively. I don't suppose I'd like it much if no one grieved at all.

I guess I should have spoken up right then and there but I couldn't, not on a busy Boston street — about a quarter looped and with a perfect stranger there, however aimiable. We started down Winter Street to Winter Place and Len took my hand . . . "Mum's the word," he said, which sounded more like the old Len. But then he added something I didn't much like the sound of.

"He'll get through all right," he said. "They all do when they want something."

Now hear the father mourning for the son . . .

Oh Charley, I hope you're not alone up there. I hope you found a whole bunch of freakouts, acidheads, frightened failures. I don't care who they are; so that they love you.

24

I DID MY DAMNDEST to keep up with Marta, scampering after her as I seldom have to scamper after anyone. Gay has to scamper to keep up with me, but then my legs are longer. Long as Marta's, but she has the advantage of not having smoked or lived as long. I cannot imagine why we were hurrying that short block; nobody else was. Perhaps she felt we had wasted enough time, or perhaps she was concerned about our reservations.

I have to admit, Marta is a fine looking young woman. She carries her small shining head and her shoulders well and she is, I think, the kind of woman with whom any man would be proud to be seen drinking and with whom any woman would be annoyed. That is because she doesn't, I think, care for women. She has a way of looking silently at you as if you have said something silly. Well, many of us often do say something silly. But Gay and I have always felt we were exceptions to the rule.

And yet all evening our contributions had been received without enthusiasm. Then Marta would address herself to Len. I admire Len — indeed I truly do — but

I am not willing to believe that intellectually, he has outdistanced us that much.

Of course, we have nothing to offer her.

One of the pleasantest memories I have is of an offensive cat that Sam and I once knew who so much trusted in her feline grace that she never looked where she was going. One day when we were watching, she fell flat on her face, a happy event we are not likely to forget. Scuttling behind her, I wished that Marta would twist one of her tall heels. Fat chance.

Boston is dying like most of the cities, more's the pity. Everyone's gone out of town. The tweedy ladies who used to buy their suits at Filene's and their household furnishings at Jordan Marsh prefer now to shop in the suburbs. Along that short block of Winter Street that used to be lined with nice small specialty shops, I counted a broken streetlight with its shards glinting dully in the gutter, and a proliferation of dark cubbyholes that dealt in old coins and soiled stamps. The very nice upstairs restaurant where my aunt and I used to have a naughty sherry is closed and the store under it, abandoned. Behind the cracked plate glass it gapes blackly, as if it had been bombed.

I am not often timid, but I began to glance nervously at the dark narrow entrances of office buildings. Somewhere I have heard or read recently that the safest part of Boston now is the North End — little Italy. Perhaps Italian parents have more control over their young or perhaps — I don't know; I only know what I read — the Mafia discourages unprofitable and conspicuous violence.

As we turned into the narrow depths of Winter Place

and waited under the weak light at the restaurant entrance, I would have welcomed a fine, firm-minded member of the Mafia. "Do you like living in the city?" I asked, breathing fairly evenly.

"It has its advantages," she said.

I'll bet it does.

"Disadvantages, too." Her eyes flicked at me. "I've had my purse snatched twice and one time someone tried to attack me in my own vestibule."

"Goodness," I said. "What happened?"

"Nothing," she said. And I believe that, too.

However, I looked at her with a new respect. Either she has a more difficult life than she lets on or a more fertile imagination. Either is admirable and either, a bit alarming. It was also possible that she was pulling my leg, which I would not have liked.

I thought her a bit scary. I thought, *she has a lean and hungry look*. And such are dangerous.

The others rounded the corner. "Here they are," I said, relieved. "There's Gay."

"Oh yes." And Marta smiled very slightly. "Gay."

As they say in the stylish French tongue, *formidable*.

Winter Place is nothing but an alley and the façade of Locke-Ober's is one of the most unprepossessing I have ever seen. Except for the fact that it is famous, I cannot imagine why the men all want to go there, unless they really like to be charged eighty-five cents for three string beans and wish to be known as the kind of man who doesn't care what he does with eighty-five cents.

The food is said to be incomparable but about this I

wouldn't know, since we never go to Locke-Ober's except on those occasions when I don't have a very clear recollection of the food. It is enough to make any waiter surly, though I will say for Locke-Ober's that the waiters are never surly. It is a tall, attenuated building and one of the waiters told me that originally the housekeeper had an apartment on the fourth floor, and that they still bed guests up there if they become obstreperous and are known to the management. I like that.

Though come to think of it, I wonder if it's low-class to be the kind of person in whom waiters confide?

I've had a lot of excellent meals the details of which subsequently escaped me, but I do know what we ate last night at Locke-Ober's, even if we didn't get to start with the clear turtle soup. They are renowned for their turtle soup and never have it. Jam yesterday and jam tomorrow, as Alice said, but no clear turtle soup this evening.

You climb a narrow enclosed stairway to get to the dining rooms, which are small and tightly packed. Everyone has made a reservation so that they won't miss out on the chance of being burned alive. If everyone had to get down those stairs at the same time, forget it. My answer to pyrophobia is usually to have another drink. Perhaps that is Walter's answer, too. He stored his manuscript beneath his chair and gazed with intent interest at the next table.

He said, "Why, I believe those people are having martinis." And forgetting the fate of his Athenaeum card he added in amazement, "I think I'll have one too."

But I don't think it was the martinis that did the damage. I think it was the wine.

Some of us had now reached a state of mild euphoria, and some had not. Walter assured us, his nice eyes watery with sincerity, that he had never spent such an evening in his life, would not forget us, wanted us all for dinner on Saturday; would never, never leave Stevens and Sons for Random House or Little, Brown, not if they were to beg on bended knee. Gay was motherly, pointing out that the price of lobsters was ridiculous and considering the portions they served here, two orders of Chateaubriand would serve us all, a sensible suggestion seconded by Marta and rejected by Wes.

Only Len brooded.

The waiter took our order. Even at Locke-Ober's, unless you ask for a twist you get an olive.

A very proud father came and sat at the table next to us. He had two daughters with long orderly hair and pretty dresses. There was a boy, too, who wore a tie and jacket and whose hair just brushed his collar. Rather a handsome boy, though I wouldn't have given you a nickel for the blue glint in his eye. The man's wife had been brought along. Her hair was carefully arranged in such an ordinary way that one could not be sure whether it was a wig or not but if it was, it was an expensive one. Let's see, I thought. I like to play let's see. Maybe one of the girls goes to Wellesley. Maybe the boy has been accepted at Groton. They are seeing Boston to be sure it will do. Possibly they had lunch at the Parker House and they have certainly seen the Old North Church. They are not late enough to have been to the theater, so they probably went to an early movie. They probably prefer early movies. I sort of liked the father.

For some reason, Len did not. You could tell. At Locke-Ober's the tables are too close. It is the only way they can get everyone in who wants to get in, but unless you are deep in drink you hear everything that is being said, which is never offensive but is not usually amusing, either. The girls said it was awfully hot for May. The mother said it was hot in Ohio too. The father said they had all better have the lobster. The mother showed him how the menu said all lobster prices had to be raised. The father said it didn't matter, not one whit, not since they were in Boston. The mother smiled proudly and patted the older daughter's hand. She said it wouldn't be the last time they were in Boston. Well, good for them.

The boy said he didn't think much of lobster anyway; lobster's a scavenger. He said he didn't think much of Boston, either.

Len said quite clearly, "Whippersnapper."

Gay said that she would have the Vichyssoise.

Have you ever noticed what unpleasant lists are circulated about? Well, take the seven signs of cancer, and the one in your telephone directory that gives you the numbers for Fire, Police, Ambulance, Coast Guard (Search and Rescue), F.B.I. How's that for a grim reminder. And then there is the list that tells you how to know if you're an alcoholic. Do I look forward to cocktail time? Yes. Do I ever draw blanks? Not often. Well, once in a while. Do I drink in the morning? Never.

Except just the one for survival. So I'm all right. But last night I thought Len was drinking too much and — just out of friendship — I told him so.

He wasn't listening. He was glaring at the boy at the next table.

And he said, "We didn't beat them enough."

Oh Len, what did you mean by enough?

Somebody wise has said that you should never strike a child except in anger. Somebody wiser might add that you cannot strike a child unless you are angry, and that the anger is always born of anguish.

At one time Len and Gay lived across from a house with a high retaining wall along which any child would be compelled to walk. Charley was strictly forbidden to go near that property for reasons that he understood — that wall was dangerous — and for reasons that he must have sensed: Len didn't like the owner of the wall, who was house-proud and feisty. He drove dogs and boys away for fear that they would damage the expensive grass that the retaining wall retained, and he had a chain across his driveway so that no one could use it in order to turn around. It must have been a nuisance to the man himself to have to let it down every time he wanted to get into his own garage, but he had paid for the blacktop and by God, no one else was going to use it.

It was a Sunday. Kids always do what they shouldn't do on Sundays. On Sundays kids get bored. This neighbor telephoned and said, "You'd better get over here. I think your kid is hurt."

I forget how old Charley was but I think about eight;

you forget how small kids are at eight. He was small enough so that Len came back across the street with his son cradled in his arms. Charley was hurt all right but we couldn't be sure how or even what had happened. The boys he'd been playing with had prudently scattered like quicksilver. Len stretched him on the sofa.

"Where does it hurt?" he asked.

Charley was conscious, just. I remember thinking that his lashes looked like ink-strokes because there was no color in his face at all. He said, "My stomach hurts."

Len pulled the dirty jersey up and eased his shorts down and then he said "Oh God. Gay, get the doctor."

But it was I who had to call because Gay, who had the shortsighted, deeply held, belief that a child should see no emotion except for joy, had fled and was sitting at the kitchen table with her wet forehead in her hands.

It was a nasty-looking cut, a four-inch opening clean and precise as a diagram; the abdominal wall had simply split. There was surprisingly little blood, but under the thin white layer of fat the exposed muscle was fibered red and deeply uncovered. The pediatrician marveled. He said that Charley must have so strained against the fall that he had burst.

He said, "Charley, this is going to hurt."

Charley said, "OK."

"So I am going to give you a shot."

Charley said, "OK."

Mothers are good but fathers are wonderful. Gay and I delegated authority to the men and looked away, but Len watched while the wound was closed and it was Len who nodded when the doctor said, "He won't be out long. Keep him quiet." And who, when the stitches were in, carried him up the stairs while Gay scuttled ahead to open up his bed.

We three sat there waiting for him to wake. It was a nice room; Gay had taken trouble with it. Three of the walls were papered with horses and saddles and the fourth was lined with low white shelves which contained many curious things. His books, of course, but an old orange, too, gone to that musty green that old oranges get to, and one of those yellow and blue kerchiefs, knotted and creased, that Cub Scouts wear. Two gull's feathers in a tomato can. And a steam engine into which Charley had all too clearly introduced ink.

The closet door was open. The closet floor was littered with vile sneakers and scuffed brown school shoes and in one corner was a big stuffed elephant limp with years that Charley would now neither recognize nor relinquish.

We waited until his lashes fluttered and then until his eyes opened and then until he tried to sit up. Gay put her hands upon his shoulders.

"No," she said gently. "You're going to have to lie there quite a while."

Then Len stood up and for the first time, started to shake. He knotted his fists to conceal it. And then with his voice thick with rage and with relief, he spoke to his son.

He said, "And when you do get out of that bed, I am going to beat the hell out of you."

Their eyes locked coldly.

"OK," Charley said.

I am sure Len never touched him, because by the time he did get out of that bed Len, of course, was all past his fear. But it was a bad cut. Charley still has the scar.

All this went through my mind in the time it took me to lean for Wes to light my cigarette. Then, meaning to be of comfort, I think I said, "Oh, Len, of course you beat him enough."

I think I said that. After such evenings one is not always sure. I once knew a stately woman who spent an entire night knocking the husband of a mutual acquaintance while the mutual acquaintance giggled with gratitude. In the morning this stately person drew herself up and said "At least, thank God, I've never told her what I think of him."

So I'm not sure. But I think I said that to Len.

25

BOTH Wes and Len are great believers in wine, which they consider civilized and a great way to get from cocktails into dinner. Since most of us had decided on snails and all of us on steak, we had to start with white and shift to red; I found that pleasant. At Locke-Ober's you pay for everything separately and the escargots come high. But I had reached that moment of peace: I was calm, able to understand it all and to forgive. I recognized that part of what you pay for at Locke-Ober's is the high prices.

And I sent good thoughts to Sam, waiting anxiously on the other coast, and I was so touched by the essential goodness of us all that I damned near asked for the telephone and called him — except that I've been at this long enough to know this moment is often the eye of the storm. I did not wish to be incoherent when I spoke to him. Or to cry: this is a dangerous stage.

Delightful, too. The rest of the room shrinks away, leaving an island to which servitors come and go while we happy few exchange what Charley once called "pro-foundies." Every word that fell from my lips was golden, and the right person caught every golden word. And the one whom I wished to harvest my wisdom did, and the person I didn't want to benefit didn't benefit.

Unfortunately there is often a specter at these feasts; last night, it was Marta. The gin she had consumed seemed only to have increased her vigilance. She had begun to watch Len with a wary eye, and it was not really up to her to remind him to use his napkin. I resented it.

I have this gift which is often (not always) operative; I can quell. I raise my brows and meet people's eyes directly, with a small cynical smile. You'd be surprised how fast it brings them down. So last night I quelled Marta, or I tried to.

"Do you know Charley?" I asked her. "Or do you know John?"

"No," she said with indifference, "I don't."

"Then you don't really know Len very well," I said, "do you."

She does not often show amusement. "Oh, well enough," she said, and I'm afraid she was amused.

She doesn't really quell all that easily.

So then I tried to feel sorry for her, because when you feel sorry for people they don't spook you so much. I thought of her as essentially homeless and manless, with only the thin comfort of a job, caught in the Limberlost between two generations, with a barrier of age on either side. It didn't work because I caught a glance that she and Len exchanged, and there was no barrier between them worth the mentioning.

Well, the hell with her.

I had reached the hour toward which it is all directed, the apogee of ease. Now from my lips would fall only rubies and roses.

Item: I said to Gay (ah, but not critically), "What's the matter with everyone? I don't mean just them, but us. Why can't anyone get by anymore without palliatives?"

And Gay agreed. "Like tonight," she said.

"Or love," I said.

"Or books."

At this stage there is a storm of food and plates are changed before you without human hands. You have to be awfully careful with your fork. At this stage I love everyone. My love is Christlike. I *am* compassion.

I looked at Walter and it seemed to me he was some kind of saint, because of all of us he was wound up with his own achievement, which is the best windup there is — but since he had flatly refused to switch to wine I leaned to him (ever so tenderly because of my loving-kindness) and told him to guard his Athenaeum card.

Those gentle, myopic eyes swam with sudden tears (perhaps after all, he *is* some kind of saint) and he said, "You are a very nice woman."

"Yes," I said. "I know."

Whoops. Watch it.

Pass the bottle . . .

By now we had had the snails and the black olives and

the carrot curls (nobody ever wants the carrot curls) and the substitute for the clear turtle soup, and I suppose the steaks must have been just grand. Gay certainly thought so.

But then the waiter was standing at Len's shoulder, our very own waiter who up until now had been so nice, and he apparently had spoken more than once.

There was a call for Len.

When he came back from that phone call I knew there was going to be trouble, although I certainly didn't spot what kind of trouble it was going to be. His face was bleached.

Gay looked up with the instant recognition that wives have.

"No," Len told her, "it's all right. Something came up about the neighbors." Which I thought masterly, because there was just enough suggestion of the unpleasant to make it credible to her. He slid into his chair, turned to me and mouthed, "Police."

Which probably meant that Charley was in jail. Well, that can mean anything these days. Cohabitation, indecent exposure, indigence. Bombing, rioting, using or selling. Sass.

Wes lifted the wine from its basket. Gay raised her bright head and said, "Well, I believe I will." In Walter's nice round face, like Mr. Pickwick's, the bright light of intelligence flickered but feebly.

Len downed a glass of wine and went to pieces right before our eyes.

The worst thing on these unfortunate occasions is the

wonderful food that nobody ever remembers. I am sure the steaks must have been superb, brown and crusty on the outside and on the inside a pale, juicy rose. But no one had eaten more than about an inch. The salads looked as if they had been toyed with and true enough, they had. The butter was melting and the hot rolls cold. Forget the vegetables.

Walter beamed on us all.

But then that miserable blue-eyed boy at the next table had to speak up, and did so in the kind of sudden silence that happens now and then. Gay had begun to worry about Len and so had Marta; their eyes were quick and alert as mice. Anyway, what the boy said was not all that bad.

He said, "Boy. All those creeps on the Common."

Len said in a clear and audible tone, "Pipsqueak." And then he arose and attempted to overturn their table.

He couldn't, really, because they hung on to it. Gay was at his side in an instant and so was the *maitre d'*, having been trained to be alert for just this sort of thing. But Len did get the tablecloth before they could intervene and the glasses and silver chattered everywhere. The family from Ohio huffed and left, but they were about to leave anyway. A few strawberries rolled at random and the wife did have some coffee on her skirt, and there was some broken glass; that was about the size of it. But the waiters were annoyed. I suppose they'd about had it for the day.

Our waiter, who had turned quite unfriendly, suggested that perhaps the gentleman was ready to retire.

This seemed a capital idea to me and I asked about the room on the fourth floor, but he said it was already occupied.

Gay said, "This is dementia."

I don't know who paid, though I assume that it was Wes, and I have no idea who left the tip. One thing I do remember — and will for a little while — was Gay's prudence and husbandry. I think she was still worrying about what John had found to eat. At any rate, she gathered Walter's manuscript and all the steaks and placed them in one of the linen napkins and then, grasping her carryall, she looked with real disapproval at the waiters. Then we departed. I wondered if they were going to speak about the napkin, but I guess they were just glad to see us go.

In the alley Len breathed as if he had been running.

"Let's walk," he said. "I think I need the walk."

Years ago when Boston was very staid and quiet and all of us were nervous because we didn't know what was going to come next, we once went wandering late at night.

It was May that time, too, the new leaves were rustling on the Common and the gas fumes hung light on the warm dark air. We got lost down around the docks where all the warehouses look alike and all the streets are alleys and we never did find the joint we were looking for, but we did find a pleasant drunk and a kindly cop. The two of them conferred, and they decided we'd do better at a Waldorf, because it was open all night and what's more, we could find it, so that's where we ended. It was bald and bright and, at that hour, smelled of disinfectant and you had to have little tickets for your coats and little tickets for your trays. Len lost some of ours, but the elderly girl let us have our coats back anyway. The pancakes were good.

I think Len thought it was still like that — Boston, I mean.

But right there in the alley, everything broke loose.

There was a black boy waiting for us. I'm sorry. I'm *sorry*, but he was black. He wasn't much more than a boy though he was a big boy, and he wasn't easy to see, but he did try to get Marta's purse, which he didn't succeed in doing because Marta, you bet your boots, never gives up anything easily. We asked for it, you know. Anyone who pays a hundred dollars for a dinner that nobody eats and then wanders, smashed, into the dark, is asking for it. How about that for conspicuous consumption?

There was a moment in which nothing was very clear to me except Marta's thumping and bumping, and then Wes said something loud and fairly sober, and the boy started to run.

I don't remember Walter's being there at all. As a matter of fact, we never saw Walter again.

Len said, "I personally am going to get the son-of-a-bitch," and he took off up Winter Street with the rest of us hightailing it behind him. Talk about your St. Walpurgis night. Wes was already out of breath, being out of training for this sort of thing. Gay was running freely and easily, though not for a moment did she let go of the carryall. Marta and I brought up the rear.

Picture those streets that in the day brim with people

shoving and pushing their way along after their many goals: last night they were black pen-strokes on moon-pale canvas. Echoing. Empty. No traffic sounds, only the staccato of our feet and the rattle of a can that someone kicked. Len turned right on Tremont and we followed him past the church and into the Old Granary Burial Ground.

That is a pleasant place, by day, a cup of quiet there in the city's hubbub where the wind blows in the grass and the bees brawl. A few tourists wander there, awed by the dates on the old sunken stones and a few clerks from the neighboring office buildings bring their lunch.

The gate was closed but the boy went over the fence like a black shadow flowing and Len lunged after him in a way that for a horrid moment made me think he would impale himself on the iron spikes. It took the rest of us a little longer, scrambling and boosting one another.

There was something wild and Halloweenish about the whole affair, and as we went leaping among the gravestones I remember thinking, "Good God. There's Paul Revere." It was very beautiful, if everyone had just stopped wrestling. The stones glimmered in the moon-light and the wrought-iron fences cast sophisticated shadows on the innocent dead. But then there were two shadows tangled in a corner and the dull belt of fists on flesh.

Gay said "Jesus, Mary and Joseph." Which is not a phrase I would think she would know (one never really knows anyone, does one) but I expect everyone around

Boston knows that phrase. Then she knotted her hands at her mouth and said, "He's only a child."

And then, thank God, there was a cop.

We waited just long enough to see his uniform, less blue than the shadows, and the glint of brass. Then Gay said, "Let's get out of here."

"Suits me," I said.

I suppose the Garden is a foolish place for two women to be, that close to midnight and all alone. But we didn't feel that way. The lacy light swayed over the paths and the few couples we passed murmured softly. At the end of the swan-pond the great wooden birds bumped gently. The water glittered and you couldn't see the floating cigarette butts and the peanut shells.

Gay said, "Let's sit down."

I said, "Suits me."

The benches are not really comfortable. Naturally the authorities do not wish to encourage couples to sit too long upon the benches, especially after dark. The moonlight through the leaves shifted the shadows at our feet.

Gay said, "What went wrong?"

I thought about it, because it was something I would like to know, too, though I think she was thinking about the evening, and I was thinking about much more than that.

I told her, "I don't think anything went wrong. There's been a lot of trouble. There's been a lot of good stuff, too."

Gay said, "I may have to leave Len. I find I'm not the sort to share a husband."

So after all, while I have been so arch and silent, she has known all along.

She always surprises me. She said, "Do you have a cigarette?"

I always have a cigarette.

Gay drew upon it gingerly and said, "You lose them just by always being there."

That's not how I lost mine. But I knew what she meant. She meant that after the orange juice and the Aureomycin and the diapers, and after the PTA and the nights when the Cub Scout pack meets with Akela, a nice man who is manager of the First National, and after the high temperatures and the smell of mumps and measles and the towers of dishes and the seas of sheets and even if it is still fine in bed, you are no more his lover but, at the best, a comfort and convenience.

Gay said, for the first time sulky as a child, "I could have gone to graduate school."

The breeze was not as gentle now as it had been, but was tempered by the cold waters of the bay. Indeed, she could have gone to graduate school.

"Well," she demanded, "what would you do?"

What would I do? Oh, boy. How do I know? If Barry had lived and I had had a son, I might still have been sitting here with Gay on that bench that is not easy on the bottom. I might by now have found even Barry only a convenience. Suddenly I felt very drunk in a bad way; my mind was clicking clearly enough but when I tried to light a cigarette I didn't make it.

We all smoke too much, anyway. Now wait a minute.
If I had had a daughter I would have told her all the
things my aunt told me. And some other things.

Don't think you understand anyone. You
don't understand anyone.
Be generous with your man.

"For your own good . . ." Gay said.

Some say the worst thing you can hear in the English
tongue is "Oh-oh," but I am partial to "For your own
good."

"Sam may have to leave you, too," Gay said.

No, Sam won't leave me. But in a way, she's right.
Sam is a good man who loves me. He wants to see me
happy and insured and if he could do it, I would be
insured and happy. And I have not been generous with
him. I have not even tried to be his lover.

Of course Gay and I have had words from time to
time, but I didn't mean what I said then as having words.

"For *your* own good," I told her. "You shouldn't
leave Len at all. You've left him quite a lot, in one way
or another."

"Maybe so," she said thoughtfully.

Both of us shivered. It was suddenly cold. So we
linked arms and slowly — not to create a draft — we
walked back to the Ritz.

26

THE DOORMAN was not surprised to see us shivering and unescorted. He is hired not to be surprised.

I don't care how grand hotels are, at that hour of night hotels are bleak. The few visible guests spoke in subdued voices; they all seemed to be engaged with tomorrow's early start and tonight's fatigue. The Bar was closed and just outside of it whoever changes the menu under its isinglass covering was changing the menu, and I could swear that from somewhere in the vicinity of the blackened breakfast room I heard the drone of a vacuum cleaner.

There was a message for us at the desk. The message was from Marta and had obviously been telephoned because the handwriting was pure Palmer Method and Marta is too young for Palmer Method. It sounded like her, though, direct and directorial.

It said, "I have Len. Stay put."

Once in a while my friend in a good uncomplicated way gets very angry.

She said, "What in the hell did she think we were going to do?"

I giggled.

I saw the two of us meandering around Boston motiveless as moths while Marta arranged everything and saw that we were all neat and safe and were going to get to the office early. Gay did not giggle. She was still offended, and told the elevator boy goodnight in a curt voice that I'm sure made him wonder if there were smut on his white gloves.

The halls had a dim underwater light that searched out the worn places on the carpeting and on most of the doors signs hung; either the blue Do Not Disturbs or the yellow breakfast orders with the round holes that you so conveniently fit over the knob. Being a natural snoop I stopped to snoop at one of them. Coffee was checked, and grapefruit and brioche *and* hot buttered toast and orange juice, and then where (2) had been checked against marmalade it had been crossed out and (3) had been written in. They must have spent a very wholesome evening.

Gay never liked my snooping. She said, "Honest to God..."

And then it happened again.

I can't see. One moment it's all there and the next it is all splintering and sparkling and whatever I'm looking at goes up in fireworks and comes down in smoke and then for a little time there is nothing but the dull, reverberating dark.

Gay said, "Take my hand."

So she has always known this, too.

I took her hand. After a while it cleared again and I saw first the length of the hall where the fog still swirled and then the dark rectangles of the doors and then the breakfast orders hanging like little flags and then my friend's soft strong hand.

"I didn't need that last drink," I explained.

"No, you didn't," she said. "Come on, now."

Mine eyes dazzle. She died young.

But for that matter, I'm not all that young.

Gay groped in her bag and said rather crossly, "I thought you took the key."

I said, "I thought you had it."

Wes opened the door and said, "I had it."

The last time Sam was with me at the Ritz I wasn't very nice. I sulked and kept on thinking about death and dying, which are not the same. The day before you go into a hospital is the longest day of the world, and Sam wouldn't let me make it a holiday. He kept insisting that I rest; at such times there is no rest, there is only lying still and looking into the future. I wanted the day bright and cluttered and speeding fast and Sam would not permit it. He counted and spaced my drinks and vetoed wine at dinner though he did let me have one liqueur. So the slow day crept and the interminable night began.

I wanted to walk, I wanted to wander, I wanted to see sights and hear music. They never do anything the first day. Twenty-hour hours in a johnny in a hospital bed is enough rest for anyone.

"We are not going to take any chance," he said.

So I stood for a long time at the window and refused all comfort.

"Oh, my love," he said.

I don't know at what point he got the key, but wherever Wes wants to get in, he gets in. The lamps were lighted and the false fire glowed in the fireplace and on the coffee table there was Irish coffee, hot and pungent, although with all due respect I have never before seen it served in brandy snifters. I must say it was comforting, although Wes himself looked tired and had that light green look that I associate with collapse. I told him that I thought he should call it a day and I think he would have, too, except that right then we were interrupted.

Because after all, Marta did not have Len.

He looked, as my aunt would have said, like the wrath of the living God. Marta had done the best she could. The cuts were covered with Band-Aids and she had tried to wash the blood from his lips, but he had bled again and his mouth was caked and swollen. And what the office is going to think about that eye, I do not know. Perhaps he can blame it on some author.

When he started throwing the glasses I made sure I finished mine before he got to it. Waste not, want not. He was berserk but methodical. One after another the glasses smashed in the fireplace in a travesty of some terrible toast.

"Well," he said at last, "they got him. The bastards got him."

But Charley wasn't dead. And it wasn't the police that got him and it wasn't his peers and it wasn't any mistake he may have made — it was Fate, it was Clotho, it was blind and brutal chance; it was a truck that broke out of hand and mounted the sidewalk and, in a horrible marriage, pinned him against the wall.

It didn't have anything to do with anything: it just happened.

There wasn't anything Wes could do except, Gay said, to get Len to bed. And then I called the airport. Gay sat there with her hands folded in her lap. There was no flight until morning.

"It's all right," she said at last. "We are too drunk to do anything tonight."

Of course we didn't sleep. The maid had turned the covers down and we took off our shoes and lay upon the beds. It was late. No, it was early. The first grey light leaked past the air conditioner.

Gay said, "I've always liked you."

I said, "I've always liked you, too."

We have done those things which we ought not to have done. The memory is grievous. The burden is intolerable. I know the desperate desire to be shriven at the cost of others is impure. Strong, though. I think it accounts for the success of the Church which allows one — no, compels one — to dump the sorry saga on a priest, who can bear the wounds of the body of Christ, because his interest is only academic.

Besides, guilt sucks away one's strength — one's *virtue*. Because of the day that was to come, I had to be absolved. So while the sky greyed over the Boston Public Garden, I tried to tell my friend that I had once slept with her husband.

Gay sighed. Then she said, "Yes, I know."

It all came back, the sickness and the smell of warm gin and the tangle of my own feet and the terrible sense that one has seen God. Gay's slim hard arm, her fierce whisper. "You are not drunk. You are faint."

"How did you know?" I asked.

She said, "You told me at the time."

So she absolved me.

While Gay slept fitfully — I think at last she slept; no matter what, one always does — I watched the dawn on the Garden. First, like a woodcut, the branches and the boughs stood out and then the black strokes of the ornamental iron gates. Then the Pond glimmered and shone whitely, there were no colors yet. I got up very quietly and sat by the window and counted up my scars. This is an interesting thing to do.

Beyond the day's bumps and bruises and the shallow cuts that will probably heal, there are the others. The tiny white line on my hand commemorates the time my Pomeranian bit me. Do you remember Pomeranians? It certainly is not disfiguring, but it taught me a lot about man's best friend and a little about love and loyalty.

And then there is my vaccination. Nowadays they don't leave marks, but you used to get a shiny place the size of a half dollar with pucker-dots all around. The doctor asked you if you would rather have it on your thigh so that it wouldn't show. Nothing is the same.

Then there's the place where I pitched into a door and sliced my nose, and the one where I tried to drink from a shattered glass, being more provident than practical. It somewhat changed my expression, but I choose to think the new expression interesting. We have to make these choices.

My broken arm doesn't show although (sometimes) it aches. It does show where I walked into barbed wire, but that was because I was reading at the time. And my hair hides where the first incision was, though it was a long time growing out. I'm not sure I want to go through all that again.

The worst scars don't show at all, but you can learn to live with them. Believe me.

I eased back on my bed and lay there listening to silence and picturing how on the bench where we had sat the dew was beading on the boards, and how it all turns out differently than you think, and then for some reason I thought of Byron, who minded his clubfoot so much.

*So we'll go no more a-roving/So late into the night
Though the heart be still as loving/And the moon be still
as bright . . .*

He hit it right on the nose.

So I watched the window brighten from pearl to gold and faced a few facts. We will go no more a-roving.

Well, all right.

Then for a little while, I think, I slept.

When we awoke the grey merciful light was gone and the room filled with the strum of traffic and the hot yellow of another day. Trays were clashing in the halls and elevators whining and somebody laughed, which was unforgivable. But the new yellow day always comes and you always have to meet it. While Gay showered I wandered through the sitting room that sparkled with broken glass, and there in Gay's straw carryall safe and sound was Walter's manuscript. It was all covered with steer's blood.

Charley was still alive.

Wes knocked and stood there looking at all the mayhem and the bloody pages that Gay, even at such a time, was trying to dry. He rubbed his head and said in a phrase we'd always liked, "What was all that tarry-hooting about last night?"

And then, God-damn, the waiter brought the breakfast. It is always a mistake to order breakfast the night before if you don't know what's going to happen before breakfast. It arrives with a round table and a fair white cloth, with fruit embedded in ice like shattered glass. The coffee is piping hot, and then there is this one lush, perfect, contemptuous rose.

And then Len came. He looked grey, frightened. And old. If he knew Wes and I were there, it didn't matter. He spoke only to his wife.

He said, "Don't ever leave me."

"No," she said. "I won't."

After such moments, what?

I said, "If we had some tomato juice, we could have a Bloody Mary if we had some gin."

"I happen to have some gin," Wes said modestly.

Gay called room service. Her face was carved with grief, but she had hold of her husband's hand. The thing is that there is no use in saying you are going to do this or do that. Things are the way they are and the way they are is how you have to face them. Or anyway, most people have to.

She said, "Three orders of tomato juice."

I raised my brows and my friend saw me raise them, and she said, "Make that four."

So then I said, "It's all going to be all right."

It is, too. Charley is not going to die. I won't have it.

Parting is always painful. Gay said, "Keep well."

"You too," I said.

And then she said a nice thing. She said, "You'll be all right. A brave heart and a courteous tongue have carried you far through the jungle."

And Gay didn't even know where I was going.

Wes called for a boy to take the luggage and he said that he would deal with the desk and that with his own hands he would get the manuscript to Stevens and Sons, and that he would tell Marta anything that Marta needed to know. And he put me in a cab and kissed me lightly and turned away so that he wouldn't hear the address I gave.

Wes is a nice man.

So here I am again. The room is very white and the bed very high and narrow and by the time you have dealt with all the papers and the next-of-kin, you are ready for the bed. That first day, you have a lot of time to think.

What I am going to do.

This time I'm going straight to the Head of the Firm, and I am going to remind him that I have never asked anything before, at least not of him. And I am going to tell him that on the whole I have had a delightful time and have enjoyed every minute of it, though perhaps some more than others, so he can forget about me. Then I am going to point out that Charley hasn't had a whack yet at anything.

I think he'll understand.

So that is what I am about to do. And then I will call Sam.